Roses are for Romance

By Jacquelyn Webb

Writers Exchange E-Publishing

http://www.writers-exchange.com/

ROSES ARE FOR ROMANCE

Chapter 1

arilyn Land, only child and partner of Tom Land, Florist, brought the van to a shuddering stop. It was just on dawn, the road deserted. In one direction loomed the Dandenong Ranges, in the other, the city of Melbourne. Trees lining the road stood as silent witnesses, looking dark and menacing. The kookaburras had begun their raucous chorus to the new day. In the other direction, a pool of reflected light against the sky marked the city of Melbourne. The road was deserted.

With a quiet oath, Marilyn climbed from the van to survey the damage. She was not unduly surprised by the flat tire - occasional punctures had to be expected when the tires were so worn - but it was getting her day off to a bad start. Since her father's heart attack, she did the deliveries as well as all the flower arrangements. And today she had to cater for three weddings.

With a shrug, she reached for the tire lever and pried off the hubcap. The skies were lightening and the rusty lugnuts stood out distinctly. Marilyn removed them, dropping each into the hubcap. She fit the jack into place and wound it up, her worries renewed about the family finances.

Although their shop was kept busy, they never seemed to have enough money left over to cover extras. The business needed a new van and someone to do the deliveries, even on a part time basis. Merry's day was getting longer and longer, as she struggled to cope.

She straightened and stared absently at the spinning wheel. The van was well canted off the ground. She wound the jack down until the wheel touched the ground again, and reached for the tire lever to prise off the hubcap.

She usually enjoyed the quiet early morning drive down from the hills, but for some reason she felt depressed. It wasn't just the flat tire, or the fact that the business was going downhill. Perhaps it was the last wedding she did? It had been a pretty wedding. The pink of the flowers matched the pink cheeks of bride; the groom was protective and adoring. They were so touchingly in love that Merry was almost envious.

Merry was twenty years old, in vital good health, and loved every minute of her job as working partner in the business. She loved her father, and Aunt Adelaide, who kept house for them all those years since her mother died, but sometimes when she saw a bridal couple who were so obviously special to each other, an inexplicable ache was set up in her heart.

A florist's shop was full of romance, the lingering perfume of love affairs; deliveries of long-stemmed roses, flower arrangements for weddings and receptions, sprays, bouquets and buttonholes for everyone. Roses are for romance, but always for other people.

Florists rose before dawn, to collect, arrange and sell flowers. Merry sighed. They were also in bed before any normal social lives started. Merry had lots of friends, but these days, with the extra work of the shop she rarely saw them.

"Need a hand?"

Merry grabbed for the tire lever and spun around like a startled cat. The country roads were lonely and sometimes not very safe. The grey bulk of a Mercedes had pulled in behind her, and the slanting rays of the early morning sun gleamed on the black hair of the tall man watching her. The car had purred to a stop so quietly that she hadn't heard it over the morning racket of the birds.

"Yes, thank you," she replied, still wary despite the well-cut sports jacket and tailored slacks.

"Try not to get grease on my jacket, there's a good girl," he warned, as he folded his jacket across her arm.

Merry's cheeks went very pink. She was suddenly aware of her appearance. She was a slightly-built, small girl who looked even smaller in her shabby black sneakers and jeans, and raggy jumper.

She watched in silence as the tall man briskly changed the tire. Muscles rippled under his silk shirt as he slid the flat under the floor of the van and shrugged his jacket back on. His face looked good-humoured, and the sun lit gold-flecked grey eyes.

"You want to dodge the city, little girl," he drawled. "Police are clamping right down on underage drivers." He got back into the Mercedes and it purred quietly into life.

The grey car dwindled down the straight road. Merry stamped her foot in frustration. "I am not an under-age driver," she yelled at the departing car. It really was too bad, that she, a working partner in her own business, should be taken for an underage child!

She climbed into the van, caught a glimpse of herself in the mirror and suddenly grinned. With her wide blue eyes, no make-up, grease smeared across her face, and soft, gold brown hair tumbled down her back, a casual passerby could be mistaken about her age.

The van puttered its steady way along the highway. Merry bit her lip as she looked at her watch. She was going to have a busy morning! She unloaded the flowers at the shop, set up the widow display, dropped the flat tire into the garage, and went home for breakfast.

"You're late, dear," Aunt Adelaide complained as she came in.

"Sorry, Aunt," Merry apologized.

She had a quick shower and changed into a skirt and blouse. After she had shrugged on her loose blue smock, brushed her hair into order, and tied it back with a matching blue ribbon, she remembered the stranger's remark about her being an underage driver. She took a deep breath and applied her make-up ruthlessly.

She gave a satisfied nod at the attractive reflection in the mirror. Underage kid indeed! She looked very poised and sophisticated, and ready to face the next part of her day.

Her father looked up from some papers he was studying as she entered the kitchen. He glanced at the clock, and the lines of worry on his face deepened.

"Trouble?"

"Flat tire," Merry explained. "No problems, Dad."

She knew exactly what he was thinking. He hated her doing that early morning run. It was a lonely trip up into the hills in the darkness before dawn. For a while he had insisted on coming with her, but he really needed to rest, and as she kept telling him, she was quite capable of driving up and back without a babysitter. It wasn't heavy work. The flowers were ready to be loaded into the van when she arrived. It was just that they had to be collected before dawn to be fresh for the day's trade.

Her father sighed and put his papers aside. He was a short, stockily built man, with a shock of grey hair and the same widely spaced blue eyes as his daughter. "I've got an appointment with the accountant and bank manager this morning. I'll see you later this afternoon."

Merry nodded agreement and reached for another cup of tea. She was aware of how slim a margin of profit they worked on. If her father could ease some money out of the bank manager, perhaps they could trade the van in for something reliable.

It was nearly noon by the time Merry had prepared and packed the flowers into the van for the deliveries. Aunt Adelaide waited on the high stool behind the counter, the boxed flowers for the weddings stacked up beside her, sorting out addresses in her neat handwriting.

Merry sighed as she waved goodbye and drove into the heavy traffic. She had three churches to decorate, two reception rooms and one private home. After that, her day was her own.

It was well after four in the afternoon before she got back. Aunt Adelaide took one look at her and made disapproving noises. "This business of working through without lunch is ridiculous," she scolded. "I've been keeping some soup hot for you."

"Just something to drink," Merry pleaded. "I think I'm too tired to even eat."

However, she let Aunt Adelaide bully her into eating the soup and putting her feet up while she drank her tea. Gradually, she relaxed. It had been a good day. Most of the tastefully arranged banks of flowers in the window were sold, and the reception rooms were particularly pleased with her flower arrangements and promised her future business.

She was staring out the window when she noticed a grey Mercedes pull up outside. The door opened and her father got out.

"Goodness!" Aunt Adelaide said, peering over her cup of tea. "I do believe it is Tom! I wonder who that is with him?"

Merry propped her chin on her hands and kept watching. It was the helpful stranger who had changed her tire. Her stomach dropped in panic, but she was reassured by the cheerful expression on her father's face. Whatever his connection was with her father, it wasn't bad news. However, she was unprepared for her father's introduction.

"Adelaide, and Merry, my love," her father said, "meet our new partner, Sean Westwood. Sean, my daughter Merry, and sister Adelaide Land."

"Nice to meet you, Sean," Aunt Adelaide said with a smile.

"Westwood flowers?" Merry asked.

Westwood Flowers was a large interstate firm of florists and Merry often envied their lavish advertising and lower prices. Sean Westwood looked down at her and his grey eyes with their curious gold flecks got an amused glint in them.

"That's right, Westwood Flowers," he agreed.

Tom Land gave his daughter a sharp glance. "Sorry, love," he explained, "The accountant's option. We either merged or went bankrupt, and Sean has offered very generous conditions."

It wouldn't be a merge, it would be a takeover! Merry stared at her father. "How could you, Dad?"

"Is there a problem?" Sean Westwood asked.

"My signature isn't going on that agreement," Merry said. "I happen to be a partner as well."

"This is true," admitted her father slowly. "It hadn't occurred to me that you might not be happy about our merger. It just seemed such a good solution to our problems."

"We haven't got any problems we can't handle," Merry said.

Sean looked at her father and then back at her. "Perhaps we could discuss the partnership details, Miss Land. You might feel happier if you studied it in more detail?"

Tom Land's face cleared. "Now that might be an idea, Merry! You've got a good business head. You go over the figures with Sean."

"I'm not interested." Even to herself Merry sounded petulant.

"Just a drive up to my office to look at the figures." He sounded amused.

There were identical worried expressions on the faces of her father and Aunt Adelaide as they watched her. She flushed. She was being childish. She followed him out to the car and slid into the front seat. The car moved out into the heavy traffic, sped quietly down the road towards the inner-city area, turned into a traffic-choked narrow street and veered sharply to dive down a ramp that led under a building. The car park was large and shadowy. The Mercedes drove across the area to stop by a lift. Sean got out. He nodded to an attendant, opened the door and helped Merry out.

They stepped into the lift in silence. It hummed its way to the top floor, where he ushered Merry into a carpeted reception area. The girl at the desk smiled at him, and people working in the glassed off areas looked up curiously.

Uncomfortable at the watching eyes, Merry stalked beside her new would-be partner, aware that her blue smock was splotched and stained with her day's work. *Why hadn't she remembered to take it off?* she raged to herself.

Sean opened the door to a private office, and a pretty, dark girl, immaculate in a tailored linen suit, looked up and smiled. "Sean! There are several dire emergencies for you to handle. Are you officially in?"

"No, Jane, and I don't want to be disturbed."

He opened another door, and Merry went through ahead of him. She waited in the centre of the room upset and angry. Yet there was nothing in the room to have caused her displeasure.

The room was furnished in unobtrusive good taste; a large desk with several phones and a laptop, and three lounge chairs against panelled walls. From the window, the city spread out below them, and further across was a breathtaking vista of the bay. Against one wall, a magnificent floral arrangement was displayed to full advantage.

Sean gestured to a chair. Merry sniffed and sat down in the comfortable chair. Sean handed over a thick file. She studied the columns of figures.

"Your father took a mortgage over the house," he began, leaning over to point at the figures.

"That was to cover the hospital bills for his heart attack," Merry remembered.

"Your lease on the shop was renewed at a higher rental."

"The position was worth hanging on to."

"The position is why I am prepared to suffer a partnership," Sean explained. "Your father wasn't interested in selling outright and I don't have an outlet in that particular location."

Merry remained silent. They had received a lot of offers because of the position, but her father had never even considered them before today.

"You are nearly two months behind on your account with the farm."

"We always pay thirty days," Merry defended. "That only makes us two or three weeks behind."

Sean leaned back. His grey eyes watched her face. "Your business is barely breaking even. The only thing you have a clear title on is that heap you were driving this morning. I am treating Merriland's very generously in offering a part partnership."

Merry placed the file back on the desk and stood up. "So, Mr. Westwood, I still have no intention on putting my signature onto that agreement. We will get by without your help."

Sean sighed. "Your father is two months behind in payments on the mortgage, three months behind on his lease, and of course only two or three weeks behind on his payments to the farm. The money you are making from that shop is going on day-to-day expenses. There is no way that the bank is going to lend on that sort of scene. When Merriland's Florists goes bankrupt, the house will be sold to pay the creditors anyway." He paused before speaking again. "I could of course let you go bankrupt and buy up the business anyway."

Merry picked up the file again and again studied the figures of the bank statements, the neat lists of itemized debts, and the mortgage payments.

"We could sell the van."

"And get about three hundred dollars for it."

"We'll manage somehow. We always have." Even to herself, her voice sounded strained and unnatural.

"Possibly," was the reply, "In the past your father was healthier. Have you bothered to consider that the hard work and worry is going to aggravate his heart condition?"

Merry bent her head lower. The sheet in front of her blurred and wavered. His logic was unanswerable. It would break her father's heart to let the business go. It was his whole life. Then again, if they went bankrupt, Westwood Flowers would pick up their little business for a song. If they tried to struggle along as they had been doing, the extra work and worry could cause her father to have a relapse.

Somehow, the carpeted, beautifully furnished office was an affront to herself and her father. It was unfair that Westwood Flowers should be so successful when Merrilands was struggling to survive. It was unfair that the good-humored man facing her was in such a strong position to dictate terms.

"I hate you," she whispered, her head still lowered. She raised her head, trying to blink away her tears. "I'll sign."

He lounged back and pressed a buzzer. "Bring in the Merriland's Agreement, Jane. There's a signature to be witnessed."

The door opened, and the dark-haired girl came in with a folder. She opened it up on the desk and handed Merry a pen. Merry signed where she indicated, and watched as Jane, whose second name appeared to be Mollison signed against her name. She gave Merry a cheery smile, unfolded a copy for her to keep and headed out the door. The door shut behind her.

"I'll drop you back at the shop," Sean said, looking at his watch. He took her arm, and she wrenched herself away from him.

"I can walk without support, thank you," she said coldly.

"I'm sure you can, but now we are officially partners, drop that sulky expression," he advised. "Try to look as if you are pleased about the partnership, if only for your father's sake."

He opened the door. Merry swept out ahead of him, across the office and reception area to the lift. The way back to the Merriland's Florist's shop was passed in silence.

"Thank you for your trouble," Merry said as she opened the door of the Mercedes.

"No trouble," he replied cheerfully. "See you in the morning."

Merry slammed the car door hard as an expression of her outraged feelings, but the door muffled gently against the car body. The car accelerated smoothly away from the kerb.

Her father and Aunt Adelaide watched her entrance through the door, with identical anxious expressions. Merry managed a reassuring smile.

"No problems, Dad," she said calmly. "Sean went over the figures with me, and I'm quite sure you've made the only decision possible."

Her reward was the look of relief on Aunt Adelaide's face, and the easing of the strain and worry lines on her father's face.

"That's my girl," he smiled. "We should be able to keep the wolf from the door from now on. I think Sean has been most generous with his terms."

Merry wasn't prepared to agree to that, so she smiled and changed the subject.

Chapter 2

The next morning, however, Merry had completely forgotten the unpalatable fact of the new partnership. Something more serious was on her mind. She shook her father awake.

"Dad!" she said urgently. "The van's been stolen!"

Her father blinked, rumpled his hair, and yawned. "Oh, Merry," he sighed. "Go back to bed. Sean organized the pick-up. The flowers will be at the shop by seven thirty."

"Where's the van?" Merry demanded.

She was still reliving her panic when she had pushed the garage doors open and saw the dark bulk of the van was missing and the little blue Mini alone in the big garage.

Her father looked at the clock. It was barely four a.m. "Really, Merry! Don't you ever listen? Sean took the van last night. He's arranged to have it cleaned up and sold."

Merry glared at her father, indignation mounting. She had come in the evening before and hurried through her dinner so she could struggle her way through the Westwood-Merriland's agreement. After reluctantly deciding that the terms were reasonable enough, she had fallen into bed, setting the alarm for her early morning trip into the hills.

"You didn't tell me," she accused.

Her father huddled back into his blankets. "Thought I did," he apologized. "You were so tired last night, probably didn't sink in. Now go back to bed like a good girl."

Merry flounced back into her bedroom. She pulled her clothes off and flung herself back into bed. She was tense and bad tempered, and in no mood to sleep the few hours until daylight.

If Sean Westwood thought he was going to control Merriland's, he had another think coming. She may have been forced into the partnership, but it was a partnership, not a takeover! He had no right to arrange to have the van sold and take over the collection of the flowers without consulting her, and she would tell him so the next time they met. With that thought, she drifted into a troubled sleep.

She slept later than she intended and arrived at the shop well after Aunt Adelaide. She read the newly painted sign on the window with mounting indignation.

"Westwood and Merriland's indeed!" she raged to Aunt Adelaide, who was filling the display stand in the front. "Why not Merriland's and Westwood?"

"Because it's Westwood and Merriland's," a cheerful voice said behind her.

Merry spun around. Sean studied her from behind the boxes of seedlings he was carrying. This morning he looked younger in a polo necked sweater and jeans, his dark hair falling across his face.

"Last of the seedlings, Miss Land," he told Aunt Adelaide.

Aunt Adelaide fluttered her special smile at him, and he gave a friendly grin that made his eyes dance. He stacked the seedlings gave Merry a nod and left. This morning he was driving a long sleek van with WESTWOOD FLORISTS across its sides.

"Lovely man," Aunt Adelaide sighed, her vague blue eyes following the van as it drove off.

"He's detestable!" Merry stormed. "He's got rid of our van, and taken over the deliveries and without even consulting me!"

"But, dear," her aunt protested. "We hated you doing that pick-up every morning, the van was hardly roadworthy, and you were looking very tired. It was very sweet and thoughtful of him. You have enough to do with the orders and the flower arrangements."

Merry almost stamped her foot. Sweet and thoughtful were not the adjectives she would have applied to their new partner! It was certainly odd that both Aunt Adelaide and her father should have taken such a liking to him.

She put her head down and concentrated on transplanting the seedlings into the larger pots, while Aunt Adelaide wrote out labels. Gradually her ill temper and resentment cleared. She loved working among the plants. It was a pleasant sunny morning and at least there was a reprieve from the continual worry of making ends meet.

A few hours later, she shook her hair back from her face, stood up and stretched. She had finished.

"And that's that!" she said. "What about a cup of coffee?"

"I've just put the kettle on," Aunt Adelaide agreed from behind the partition.

A shadow lengthened across the doorway. "I hope there's one for me?" a familiar voice asked.

Merry's face dimpled into a smile. The fair-haired young man strode into the shop and pulled her off her feet to hug her. Merry returned his embrace warmly. "Welcome back, Robert," she said.

Robert Townsend grinned down at Merry without releasing her. "The prodigal returns," he announced. "I've spent three months on a fishing boat up the coast. I'm back to see the city lights, and enjoy some civilized company."

"It's you, is it Robert?" Aunt Adelaide asked, blinking at him from behind her glasses. "Suppose you'd like a cup of coffee?"

For a few seconds she sounded frosty, but Robert moved away from Merry to bend down and kiss her and she thawed. She never could resist her nephew's breezy manner, although she disapproved strongly of his lifestyle.

"Wasting his parents' money, and throwing away his chances," she always sniffed, when news of his latest escapades reached her.

Merry handed over the mug of coffee, her cheeks pink, and her eyes glowing. Robert was her very favourite cousin. His mother was a sister of Tom and Adelaide, and he always declared that they were his favourite relations, breezily ignoring the united disapproval of his aunt and uncle towards his lifestyle.

Despite the advantages of his parents' money, he had never finished his degree, never bothered to attend to the family business and drifted around the country working or idling as he felt like it. Sometimes he lazed away a summer following the surf, or went inland fruit picking, or up north on a cattle station. When he did come to Melbourne, it was always to visit the more tolerant Land family. He never kept in touch with his own family unless it was to ask for money.

"You're growing up, Merry," he teased. "Going to help me paint the town red tonight?"

"What about faint pink on Saturday night?" Merry returned. "I have to get up too early during the week."

"How long are you down for?" Aunt Adelaide asked.

Robert shrugged. For a few seconds his heavy lids hooded his bright blue eyes, blocking out the laughter, so that he looked older and more wary. "Thought I might hang around for a while," he declared. "Give you a hand in the shop."

Aunt Adelaide looked flustered. Robert was helpful some of the time, but the last time he was supposed to be helping, he went joy riding in the hills instead of finishing the deliveries. Merry stifled a giggle.

"That's awfully good of you, Robert," Merry said. "But we really start too early for you." Aunt Adelaide looked relieved.

Robert raised an eyebrow and put a coaxing arm around Merry's waist. "Shame on you, Merry! Think I can't get up early? Promise I will be here first thing in the morning, whenever that might be."

"But there won't be any need," said a brisk voice.

Merry wondered how long Sean had been listening. He leaned against the open doorway, with two bulky boxes under one arm. Robert tightened his arm around her. His eyes were very bright as he measured the other man.

"I fancy being helpful," he explained.

"This is Sean Westwood, our new partner," Aunt Adelaide introduced. "Sean, this is my nephew Robert Townsend. He's down in Melbourne for a few days."

Sean nodded, ignoring the proffered hand. "I'm sure you will be busy enough without working here." He turned his attention to Aunt Adelaide. "I thought I would drop in the new vases we're using for display in our other shops."

"Yes, they're lovely, Sean," Aunt Adelaide admired as she took the lid off the boxes.

"Robert always gives us a few days of his time when he is in Melbourne," Merry explained, completely forgetting that Robert was the last person that she ever needed to help them in the shop.

Sean glanced at Robert. "Kind of him, but quite unnecessary," he said firmly. "If the shop is shorthanded or busy, I'll send one of the boys around from one of the other shops to give you a hand."

Merry flushed. "I am a partner in the business after all. I can organize my own staffing."

Sean nodded agreement and glanced again at Robert. "No one is disputing it," he said smoothly, and turned and left, leaving Merry stranded in her argument.

Aunt Adelaide was the first to speak. "That was rude of you, Merry! I'm sure that Sean didn't mean you to interpret his offer as interference."

"But it was!" Merry pointed out. "He just tried to dictate whom we should employ."

"So that is the great Sean Westwood," Robert remarked. He looked thoughtful, almost calculating. "He looks younger than I expected."

"And what did you expect?" Merry asked crossly. "I didn't know you knew of him."

"I heard of the new partnership," Robert replied. "Who hasn't heard of the great Sean Westwood? Now what about painting the town pink Saturday night?"

"A wonderful idea," Merry agreed, ignoring Aunt Adelaide's reproving eyes. "See you on Saturday night about seven, unless you want to come in for dinner?"

Robert declined the invitation. "I have some stuff to attend to," he apologized. "See you on Saturday."

After he left, Aunt Adelaide spent some minutes fiddling with the wrapping paper before she spoke. "That Robert is a scamp, Merry. I don't think that your father would like you getting too friendly with him."

"He's my cousin," Merry defended. "And we've been friendly all my life. Why should Daddy mind?"

Aunt Adelaide was silenced, but the expression on her face was still disapproving.

The rest of the week passed smoothly enough. They saw no more of Robert, but Sean was a constant visitor to the shop. They acquired more display cases, and Sean streamlined their bookkeeping. Under Aunt Adelaide's reproachful gaze, Merry was stiltedly polite, but inwardly she fumed.

It wasn't that she could find anything wrong with his innovations, but his attitude annoyed her. Even his permanent good humour annoyed her. What had upset her even more was the way her father had taken to him and agreed wholeheartedly with all the changes he suggested.

On Saturday afternoon, Merry finished all her flower arrangements, and closed the shop up with something like relief. At least she was going to have a whole day and a half without the irritating presence of their partner.

Tom Land, on being told of Merry's date with Robert, rumpled his grey hair and sighed. "Of course, he's your cousin, Merry and he's an amusing scamp, but remember that he is a scamp."

"He is a lot more mature these days," Merry defended, then changed the subject. "You look awfully tired, Dad. Are you getting in an early night?"

"I'm dropping around to see Sean to discuss his idea of me supervising the new nursery full time, but I intend to be back early."

"Sounds like a good idea," Merry agreed.

Since Sean had suggested the new nursery, they had rarely seen her father in the shop. She knew that he was very interested in running the nursery full time. Despite her antagonism to Sean, she had to admit to herself that it was a tactful way to ease her father out of the heavier running of the shop. In the nursery, there was sufficient help for him just to have to supervise.

She glanced at the clock and flew into her bedroom to change. It was a long time since she had been out after dark. Just lately, the shop had taken every shred of her strength and energy, so she was always too tired to enjoy herself and had drifted further and further away from her particular circle of friends.

She surveyed her reflection critically. The high heels and clinging blue crepe skirt gave her height, and the strapless top made her feel sophisticated. She shrugged on the matching jacket, and carefully pinned her hair up into a more severe style. Her elegant reflection nodded approval. No one would mistake her for an underage child this evening.

"Very nice," Robert admired, as she made her entrance. He had exercised his family ties by coming quietly in the back way without knocking and waited in the lounge room with her father and Aunt Adelaide.

Aunt Adelaide looked up from her knitting. "What's keeping that top up?" she demanded.

"Really, Aunt Adelaide!" Merry replied in exasperation. "Me!"

She grabbed Robert's arm and pulled him out, before Aunt Adelaide came out with her lecture about the damage done to breasts by going without bras. Even if Robert was her cousin, she was getting too grown up for Aunt Adelaide to carry on in front of him.

"Bye, Aunt Adelaide, Dad," she called back.

"Don't be too late," were her aunt's parting words.

Merry paused to admire the red sports car parked in the street. Robert opened the door with a flourish.

"Very luxurious," she said as she nestled into the sheepskin-covered bucket seat. "Whose it is, and what is it?"

"A Lamborghini, and it belongs to a friend. I drove down from Eden in it."

"Some friend!" Merry said.

Robert slid a sidelong glance at her, and his eyes danced. "A very good friend! I am tempted to sacrifice my freedom and gratify that sour-faced pair who claim to be my parents."

"You are actually thinking of getting married?" Merry interpreted, staring at Robert in surprise.

Robert's romances were always short-lived hectic affairs. Either his choice of females outraged his family, or his escapades outraged his females. The family had long since despaired of seeing Robert get serious about a girl.

Robert grinned and concentrated on his driving. "I don't intend to do anything impulsive, but between her daddy's yacht, and very own Lamborghini, I might just get tempted."

"We would be so thrilled if you found a nice girl and got married," Merry said, ignoring the cynicism of the statement as one of Robert's poses. "Merriland's Florists could do the flowers and..."

"Westwood and Merriland's, you mean don't you?" Robert corrected.

The happy glow around Merry dimmed. She had forgotten about the new partnership.

"Cheer up," Robert soothed. "I've brought a present back for you."

Merry brightened. Robert's presents were a custom that went back to her childhood, when she faithfully wrote to her lonely cousin, unhappy at boarding school. He always arrived to visit during term holidays clutching a thank-you present for her.

"I meant to bring it with me," Robert admitted in response to the glowing, expectant look Merry gave him. "A book on Japanese flower arrangements. Give it to you tomorrow."

"Oh, Robert," Merry scolded. "I want it right now! Please! Where are you staying?"

"Majestic," Robert capitulated, as he spun the car around. "I've got a suite there for a few weeks."

"Majestic!" Merry echoed. Her eyes rounded in awe. "How much is that costing?"

"Don't fuss, Merry," Robert laughed. "It belongs to a friend. I need something to take away the smell of fish and the memory of those hard bunks and dirty blankets."

"What about when you leave here?" Merry questioned, "All that comfort is going to be easy to get used to."

"Visit the aforesaid sour-faced parents for a hand-out and move on," Robert drawled, suddenly bitter.

Merry was silenced.

His parents were not sour faced, just so bitterly disappointed in their expectations of their only son. It was a shame Robert had such a bad relationship with his parents! They had expected so much from him, choosing schools, friends and a career. He rebelled and went his own way, but their recriminations and arguments continued over his way of life.

The car threaded its way through the heavy traffic, and Merry woke from her abstracted reverie as the car pulled into an underground car park.

"Where are we?"

"The hotel car park, my love." Robert opened her door with a flourish. "We are going up to an opulent and sinful hotel suite to look at my etchings."

He twirled an imaginary moustache and leered at her over an invisible cloak. Merry giggled, and let herself be escorted up the lift and through into the comfortable sitting room. She took in the luxury of the furnishings with a disbelieving stare.

"Very indulgent," she commented.

Robert grinned and picked up the carefully wrapped parcel from the small table. "Here's your present, my love. Can we go off and start painting the town pink now?"

"In a minute," Merry promised. She sat down on the couch and carefully unwrapped the book. "Oh!" she gasped.

"I knew that would make you happy," Robert remarked in a smug tone. He took a bottle out of the refrigerator and poured out two drinks and came over and sat down beside her. "It's supposed to be a limited edition. Do you have that copy?"

"Of course not!" Merry turned the pages with a reverent hand. "It's absolutely beautiful." She sipped her drink without looking, and wrinkled her nose. "Yuk! Robert! What is it?"

"I ought to know better than waste expensive Irish Cream whisky on a peasant like you," Robert said dolefully, as he put her glass on the small table. "Now what say we go on with our painting the town pink?"

Merry smiled as she carefully slipped the book back into its wrappings again. "I think you are a real sweetie, Robert, wasting your hard-earned wages. This must have cost the earth!"

"I like wasting my substance on favourite cousins, wine and wild, wild women," he teased.

Merry giggled. Robert was only telling the truth. If he was a scamp, he was a very likable one with his impulsive generosity. Despite the fact that his family called him thriftless, careless and untrustworthy, there was something very nice about him.

She slid one arm around his neck and kissed him lightly on the cheek. "Thank you anyway, Robert. Promise I won't open the book again until we get home."

"Very good, little cousin," approved Robert, giving her shoulders a squeeze as he returned her kiss. "I'll hold you to that promise. I'll just finish my drink, and your drink and we'll get moving."

There was the sound of a key in the door and as it opened, Robert looked up. "Hello, Toni," he said amicably. "I didn't think you would get here until the morning."

There was a silence. The girl standing in the doorway looked at Merry and Robert on the couch and the two drinks in front of them. She scowled. She didn't look very friendly.

"Obviously," she sneered. "Quite a cozy little scene! Sitting in our hotel suite, drinking my Irish Cream, and driving your girlfriend around in my car. Is she going to sleep in my bed and wear my clothes as well?"

Chapter 3

"Now just a minute," Robert protested trying not to laugh.

The girl raised her voice and kept on yelling. She seemed in a furious temper. "I always picked you for a smooth, two-timing crook, but I never thought that you would have the nerve to bring your strays into our hotel suite."

Robert started to laugh outright, which enraged the girl even further. She paced up and down. She abused Robert, his character, his taste in clothes and females, and everything that he had done over the past six months.

Merry sneaked a look at Robert as the bitter tongue-lashing went on. Not only was he heaving with mirth at her wrath, but also there was an undisguised admiration and tenderness in his eyes. So this was the girl whom Robert was thinking about almost marrying!

She didn't really look Robert's type. Robert went in for super cool, blasé females. This girl was about Merry's build and radiated passion and temper, from her flying black hair to her snapping black eyes. She was definitely not the detached, cool and languid type.

"Oh, oh, you insufferable pig," the girl stormed, as she paused to take a breath.

"If you have finished making a fool of yourself, I would like you to meet my cousin Merry," Robert chuckled.

"And very close kissing cousins, you look, too. Get out of this suite and take your kissing cousin with you."

The amusement deepened on Robert's face. "But I haven't finished your excellent Irish Cream yet, darling. Do be civilized."

"Let me help you finish it," Toni snapped, as she grabbed the bottle and flung the contents over Robert and Merry.

"Oh!" Merry gasped, trying to shield her precious book as the sticky liquor trickled over her hair and splattered her top and skirt.

"Out! Out!" The girl raged, then grabbed Merry's wrist and dragged her across the room towards the door.

Robert put up a protesting hand. Merry saw with annoyance that he was so convulsed with laughter he was incapable of standing up. His silk shirt and his grey slacks were stained and dripping with the liquor, but still he laughed.

"I might have known it would be you, Toni," remarked a familiar voice. "What are you kicking up such a racket over this time?"

Sean Westwood stood in the open doorway, taking in the annoyed Merry with her dripping hair and clothes and Robert sprawled laughing on the couch. He looked amused.

Toni didn't look at all surprised to see him. "This two-timing bastard had the cheek to bring his tart up here, driving her around in my Lamborghini, and drinking my liquor in our hotel suite."

"Well, he's not two-timing you with this young woman," Sean said smoothly. "This is Merry Land, my new partner and I asked Robert to stay with her until I got back." His voice became a fraction dry. "Robert and Merry are cousins."

"Oh!" Toni said. She gave Sean a cautious look and swung around to inspect Merry. There was a calculating, enigmatic look in her black eyes.

Robert stopped laughing long enough to choke out. "That's right, Toni. Sean and her father weren't back when we arrived and I didn't want Merry to have to wait in the hotel lobby."

"Oh!" Toni said again. The bright pink faded from her cheeks, and the sparkle from her black eyes. "Darling," she cooed. "I'm so sorry I jumped to conclusions, but you know it did look awfully damning."

She went over and put her arms around Robert. Merry opened her mouth to protest it was a dreadful shameless fib. Robert caught her eye and winked broadly. Merry started to grin despite herself. It was a stupid situation! Trust Robert to behave like a scamp! It now looked as if his offer to help her paint the town pink was discarded, and her with it! This was so Robert! He had no right to involve her in his intrigues! He probably didn't care for the girl, only the fact that she was wealthy.

Almost of her own volition, the words formed on Merry's lips. She heard herself saying. "I'm terribly sorry I upset you by using your hotel suite to wait in, Toni, but Sean assured me he would only be a few minutes late."

"I didn't realize you were Sean's new partner," Toni said ungraciously. "I'm sorry I got impulsive. Send me the dry-cleaning bill."

"Off you go, Merry," Robert suggested, as he tightened his arm around Toni. "Toni and I have a lot to talk about and I have to get changed."

Merry stopped being amused. She opened her mouth indignantly, and then shut it again. What on earth did Robert expect her to do now? She was aware of Sean's warm hand under her arm as he propelled her through the door, along the passageway and through another door.

Merry came to a dead stop. It was another of the quietly elegant hotel suites. Sean gave her a small push that sent her through the door, and closed it after them.

"I do think we should have a little talk," he drawled. "And especially about your not very attentive cousin."

"What about the difficulty your friend Toni has in behaving like a lady," Merry retorted.

Sean shrugged. "Her father's Italian and her mother's Irish, and it makes a volatile combination. What's the charming Robert's excuse?"

"I'm going home," Merry announced, evading Sean's question as none of his business. "I'm a mess!"

"Your father will be here soon, so you can go home with him," Sean suggested. "You won't get a cab this hour of night and I can't leave until after my interview with your father."

"The perfect gentleman," Merry snapped. "I can't sit around for half an hour in these clothes."

"Don't carry on, there's a good girl," Sean advised as he settled himself down at the small desk in front of some papers. "Have a shower and I'll send your stuff down to be cleaned."

Merry glared at him. How very like a man to think up such a ridiculous solution! What was she supposed to do until her clothes arrived back? It wouldn't have mattered so much if it was Robert, but to be stranded half an hour without clothes with a stranger in his hotel suite would be embarrassing and uncomfortable. Come to think of it, what was he doing residing at the hotel suite? She had a vague memory that the address on the agreement was somewhere on the Peninsula.

"Why are you staying here?" she demanded before she realized how curious she sounded.

"Refuge from the decorators," he returned. "Toni certainly made a mess of you, didn't she?"

Merry was again reminded of how dreadful she must look. She pushed her hair back. It was sticky and stiff. Her pale crepe skirt was a splatter of stains. Her bodice had been protected by the jacket, but the jacket was even worse than the skirt. She stank of Irish Cream and felt horrible!

"The bathroom is through there, and if you pass out your clothes, I'll send them downstairs to be sponged off," he suggested.

Merry carefully put down her book and went into the bathroom. A white towelling shave coat hung behind the door. She stripped and wrapped it around her and took her bundled up clothes back into the lounge.

"Go and have a shower and I'll ring for room service," was all Sean said without looking up from his documents.

Merry flounced back into the bathroom, locked the door and got under the shower. She shampooed her hair and scrubbed herself down. She started to feel better as she towelled her hair dry on the fluffy white towel. Her brocade shoes were stained so she scrubbed them clean with the small nailbrush.

Afterwards she wrapped the shave coat tightly around her and ran a comb through her hair. It fell in damp ringlets down her back. The sleek, elegant, sophisticated look she had started the evening with was completely gone. She sighed, picked up her shoes, and returned to the sitting room.

"Is there anywhere I can dry my shoes?" she asked.

A man in a shabby, grey suit turned at her voice. It was her father! He gave her a blank look, taking in her still damp hair, and the bare legs under the shave coat.

"Merry?" he asked in bewilderment.

"It's all right, Dad," Merry assured him, suddenly aware that in her father's eyes it didn't look all right at all. "I had an accident with a drink and Sean let me use his bathroom to clean up."

"Where's Robert?" Tom Land demanded. His face became an alarming shade of puce.

"He should be here in a minute," Sean said smoothly. "He went in to see if Toni had changed yet. We're going to Valentinos for a while." He gestured towards a window. "Try the heating vent."

Whatever suspicion there was in Tom's eyes faded, as did his alarming puce colour. Merry placed her shoes on the vent, relieved that Robert had been saved from her father's disapproval. If he ever found out what Robert had done, he would join in the rest of the family chorus about how irresponsible Robert was.

"About this nursery," Sean said in a brisk voice.

Tom lost interest in his daughter and bent his head over the sheaf of plans and figures in front of him. Merry sat down and opened her book on Japanese Flower arrangements.

Some time later, there was a knock on the door. Merry looked up hopefully, wondering if it was her clothes, but it was Toni and Robert. Robert was changed into a fresh shirt and trousers and Toni was a vision in frothing, red chiffon. She clung to Robert's arm and flashed a radiant smile at the two men in the room.

"Hi, Uncle Tom," Robert said breezily. "I'd like you to meet Toni Gamberton."

"His new fiancé," Toni purred.

Robert looked startled for a split second and then the ready laughter was in his eyes again as he grinned down at her. "My new fiancé," he agreed.

Tom Land stood up and shook hands with the dark-haired girl and his blue eyes twinkled his pleasure. "Pleased to meet you, young lady," he said.

"I've heard such a lot about you from Sean. I didn't realize that Robert was the young man you were friendly with. He is a very lucky fellow."

Merry glanced at her father. Just what sort of things had Sean Westwood been telling her father about Toni and Robert? Was Robert really engaged to Toni? It was not like him to commit himself outright in this manner, although it was actually Toni who had committed him.

"I hope Sean wasn't too unkind?" Toni said nicely. "This makes us almost family. I didn't realize that Robert was related to you."

Tom smiled. "And I'm very pleased to be able to welcome you into the family, young lady, and I'm sure I can speak for Robert's parents as well." He glanced at his watch. "Well, Sean tells me you are all going to Valentino's for the evening, so perhaps I will meet you again some time." He got as far as the door and paused, looking at Merry. "You should have told me that you were going out in a foursome, Merry," he reproached and then shut the door quietly behind him.

While the relief was still tangible in the air, Merry took a deep breath and spoke. "Don't count me in your plans," she warned.

"Just for a little while," Robert coaxed. "For goodness sake, don't decide to beat your father home, Merry."

Merry took another deep breath to tell Robert that there were limits, even to help him with his romance, when there was a light knock on the door, and two older people swept into the room.

"We knew we would find you with Sean," the woman trilled.

Even before Toni's "Hi, Mum. Hi, Dad," Merry acknowledged the resemblance. Her mother was sleekly and expensively dressed, and her smile stopped short of the hard hazel eyes, inspecting Merry so suspiciously. Toni's black eyes were shrewd and appraising in her father's face.

"I'm not with Sean," Toni said baldly. "Merry is!" She clung even tighter to Robert's arm and slanted a mischievous look up at him. "I'm with Robert."

"This is Merry Land," Sean introduced. "Mr. and Mrs. Gamberton, Toni's parents."

"We did hear that you had taken over a small florist," the woman said dismissively. "Something to do with the position, wasn't it?"

"Not too small," Toni purred. "Hadn't you heard? Sean is engaged to Merry!"

Merry took a deep breath to deny the statement. Sean slid a brutal arm around her waist, pulling her so tightly against him that it choked off her utterance.

"We wanted a little time before announcing it, Toni," he said smoothly.

For a few seconds there was blank dismay on the parents' faces. Mrs. Gamberton was the first to recover.

"Really," she drawled, making the word as insulting as possible, as she inspected Merry's dishevelled hair tumbling down her back, and her bare legs and bare feet under the shave coat.

Merry fumed, aware that the shave coat didn't cover very much of her. Just what were Toni's parents thinking of her? Why was Sean going along with Toni's embarrassing allegation? Yet her denial would only make the situation look even worse. She struggled to move away, but Sean's arm was iron hard around her.

"And as engagements are in the air, I thought I should let you know that Robert and I are also engaged," Toni said defiantly.

The silence was suddenly horrified. Both the Gambertons glared their hatred and consternation at Robert, who gave them a broad smile.

"Really!" growled Mr. Gamberton. The indulgent smile had vanished from his face, and he looked almost dangerous. He pushed his heavy head forward to glare at Robert. "And by what right, young man, do you think you are going to become engaged to my daughter?"

"Really, Daddy," Toni said with a shrug. "Don't be so feudal."

At that moment, there was a tap on the door and Merry's clothes were passed through. Sean looked at his watch, and ushered Mr. and Mrs. Gamberton towards the door.

"We're all going to Valentino's. Perhaps you can discuss this with Robert some other time?" he suggested. He glanced down at Merry. "Do hurry up and get changed, Merry. You don't want to spoil our evening."

Merry, released from the achingly tight grip she had been held in, grabbed her clothes and fled for the security of the bathroom. Perhaps Robert had met his match in the quick-tempered and changeable Toni, but why involve her in such an awkward situation? As soon as she was dressed she promised herself, she would let them know where they stood on her phony engagement to Sean of all people. She dressed quickly. Every stain and mark had been removed successfully from her top and skirt. She started to feel more confident about her appearance. She tried to yank her tangled, curly hair into some sort of order.

Her eyes became suddenly thoughtful as she stared in the mirror. Why was it in Sean's interest to encourage the Gambertons to think he was engaged? Why had Sean backed Toni up so smoothly? She brushed her hair more slowly. She straightened her shoulders and gave up on the glossy mass of curls cascading down her back. It made her look neither elegant nor sophisticated, but she had something more important on her mind than her appearance.

She opened the bathroom door and prepared for battle. The three waiting for her were going to have to do a lot of explaining.

Chapter 4

"I don't care," Toni was saying to Sean as Merry came in. "It got them off my back for a breathing space." She looked faintly mocking. "And yours, my dear Sean! They won't be so quick to push us together if you have the protection of a fiancée."

"Not like you to be so thoughtful, Toni," Sean drawled. "You have got your parents off my back very nicely, but Merry is a bit underage to make a plausible fiancée."

"Who is breaking this engagement right now," Merry announced.

"Shortest engagement in history," Robert laughed. "And I thought it such a suitable match."

Merry glared at Robert. He grinned back at her. She felt herself dimpling. It was really hard to stay annoyed with Robert even if he had dumped her on Sean for the evening. He was behaving in his usual, irresponsible manner. What was it Aunt Adelaide always said about him? That he managed to get through life as comfortably as possible regardless of other people!

"I must congratulate you on your engagement, Robert," she cooed. "And Toni has my very best wishes for the future."

Robert's eyes hooded, but his grin was as engaging as ever. Merry knew that she had guessed accurately. Toni had jumped the gun by announcing their engagement. "We'll manage," he assured her.

"Ready, are you?" Sean asked. He looked down at Merry's glowing make-up free face and the already tangling mass of curly hair cascading down her back and grinned. "Are we still going to Valentino's to risk being thrown out? Valentino's is for an older clientele."

"We'll probably meet you there," Toni said as she put a possessive arm through Robert's and swept him out.

"Toni's my cousin," Sean explained, as he picked up his jacket and jingled his car keys. "Our mothers are very close friends. Toni Gamberton, among other things, runs one of the biggest nurseries in the state. They had hoped that Toni and I would merge the family interests by marrying."

He smiled down at Merry in a form of silent apology. It was a smile that lit his grey eyes and softened his entire face; his mouth relaxed into a mobile humorous shape.

"A bit cowardly of you to go along with it," she said primly, but her treacherous dimple appeared by the side of her mouth.

"Actually, the solution of an underage fiancée had never occurred to me," Sean mused. His smile broadened into a grin as he inspected her again. "We could be engaged for the next ten years while I waited for you to grow up. By then, someone would have taken Toni off my hands."

"Or she could be waiting to grab you between husbands," Merry ventured. "Don't you think we should get moving?"

Sean laughed at that, and they drove in a companionable silence to Valentino's. It was a very large nightclub with several floors, and as Sean had said, catered to a mainly older clientele. There was no sign of Robert or Toni, and Merry resigned herself to an evening alone with Sean.

After a while, it didn't seem so bad. He was an excellent dancer, and an attentive escort. Merry started to relax and enjoy herself. She sneaked a look at her watch and decided that soon she would be able to plead tiredness and call the evening over.

Not that it was turning out that badly. It was as if it was just being spent with an amusing, well-mannered stranger, rather than Sean Westwood of Westwood Flowers. Just then Toni, Robert and several other people swept up. They were noisy and cheerful as if they had been celebrating more freely.

"Looking for you everywhere, darlings," Toni called. Her black eyes glittered, and her face was flushed a hectic red. Robert looked sober enough, but Merry remembered he never showed the amount of drink he consumed.

"Jed, Diana, Brett, Serena," Toni introduced. "You all know Sean, and of course this is Merry, his new fiancée. A bit under-aged, but Sean believes in training them young," she finished maliciously.

"Enough's enough," Sean warned, but Toni shrugged her shoulders and gave a high-pitched giggle.

Toni, Robert and the rest of the crowd settled themselves down at the table. Merry smiled as she turned down the offer of champagne. Jed, or was it Brett, asked Merry to dance. She spent the rest of the evening dancing with the other members of their party.

Robert gave her a grin but stayed well out of her way and danced exclusively with Toni. They made a well-matched couple, Merry decided as she watched them. Toni's dark colouring looked even more striking against Robert's blond good looks and their dancing was faultless.

Jed then asked Merry to dance again. He was a heavily built man with high colour in his face and hard grey eyes. As soon as they stood up and moved together Merry realized that it was a mistake. He had drunk enough to make him clumsy on his feet and he held her more tightly than was necessary.

"Are you really Sean's partner?" he quizzed. "He sure can pick 'em."

"My father and I are in partnership with Westwood Florists," Merry replied coolly. She decided that Jed was being offensive and decided to plead tiredness and move back to the table.

"Very cute," Jed chuckled. His arms tightened even more. "You look under-age to me. Maybe we can do Sean a favour and grow you up a little." His breath was sour and acrid as he mouthed at her averted cheek.

"Mind if I cut in?" Sean interrupted and smoothly plucked Merry from Jed's arms. "Don't want to encourage him," he warned. "He's a nasty drunk."

"I wasn't encouraging him," Merry retorted, relieved to be rescued, and annoyed at Sean's assumption that she needed rescuing. "Besides, I'm tired, and I'd like to be taken home."

"Of course," Sean said smoothly.

They went back to the table. No one seemed interested in their departure. The wine and champagne were flowing very freely, and the party seated at the table sounded even more exuberant. Toni gave them a dismissing wave and Robert winked and called he would be seeing her on Monday at the shop.

Sean broke the silence of their drive home only as he opened the car door and walked her up the path. Merry noticed with exasperation that the kitchen light was still on. Aunt Adelaide, as usual, was sitting up until she got in.

"Thank you for a pleasant evening," Sean drawled.

Merry suddenly realized that their excursion to Valentino's wouldn't have been in Sean's original plans. If Toni hadn't turned up so unexpectedly, and Robert hadn't involved him, what would he have done?

"What were your plans for the evening, anyway?" Merry asked curiously.

"I would have slaved over the books," he said. His teeth flashed white in the shadowy gloom of the front veranda. "It was a pleasant break anyway. Thanks, Merry."

He bent, and for a second his warm mouth brushed Merry's lips and then he turned and strolled back to the car. Merry opened the door, and went inside, startled and puzzled by his odd gesture.

"That you, Merry?" Aunt Adelaide called.

"Back before midnight, just like Cinderella," Merry assured her and fled straight to the privacy of her bedroom.

Sean, she decided as she undressed, was an enigma and a puzzle. They were business partners, but not really friends, despite their pleasant evening. Why had he kissed her?

Chapter 5

The following week, however, the newfound tolerance of Merry to their partner plummeted to non-existence. Robert, true to his promise, had arrived at the shop on the Monday to help. Merry had sent Sean's driver back and Robert had taken over the deliveries in the big new van.

This brought Sean across to the shop to confront Merry as to why she had returned his driver. He was quite good-humoured and sounded quite reasonable, but Merry listened with mounting indignation to what he had to say.

"It's very kind of Robert to offer to help, but quite unnecessary," Sean had explained. "I prefer Merriland's to use the driver I sent over. He is conscientious and he knows the deliveries."

"Robert's just helping out as a member of the family for a while," Merry was able to explain sweetly.

"The business doesn't need the help of Robert," Sean replied. "And I like to keep the records straight on my payroll."

What Sean was hinting at ever so delicately was that he controlled the purse strings and therefore any matters of staffing Merry decided.

"So!" she retorted. "As he is not on your payroll he isn't really a member of your staff and not subject to your control, is he?"

"I have always thought that volunteer labour belongs with charity organizations, not in an efficient business," he said.

"Works quite well in family businesses," Merry replied.

"He's driving our van," he pointed out.

"Exactly!" Merry smiled as she regained her temper. "I assume that you are referring to the Westward and Merriland's van? I did understand that it was to do the deliveries from this particular shop?" Her voice sharpened, "Especially as you took it upon yourself to sell our van without consulting me!"

"That death trap! It practically cost money to get the wreckers to take it." He looked at his watch. "I hope your volunteer labour proves satisfactory," he said and strode off.

Merry watched him go with satisfaction. The trouble with people like Sean Westwood was that they became too used to getting their own way and assumed that they had a God given right to trample ruthlessly over other people's wishes.

"I don't know, dear," Aunt Adelaide said as the Mercedes drove away. She looked worried. "Don't you think it was a bit silly to stick your neck out? I mean, you know Robert!"

"Nonsense!" Merry said. "Robert has outgrown his irresponsible streak. After all, he has just become engaged. He wouldn't do anything silly these days."

Aunt Adelaide shook her head in disbelief. Merry thought for a brief second that if Sean hadn't been so pushy, she wouldn't have been moved to defend Robert so hotly. She was very much aware of Robert's couldn't-care-less attitude to anything to be taken seriously. Therefore, she was both pleased and relieved at how hard Robert worked for the next few days.

Besides, it was a pleasure having him in and out of the shop, with his easy-going grin and his continuous teasing. Even Aunt Adelaide laughed out loud at his cheeky comments and Merry relaxed even more. Robert had surely outgrown the irresponsible streak, and he was being very helpful. However, on Thursday afternoon, he didn't return from the afternoon round.

"Where can he be?" Aunt Adelaide asked crossly. "I wanted him to drop this extra order off."

"Maybe he got caught up," Merry placated. "You know Robert! I'll drop the order off with the Mini on the way home."

Robert was a very hard worker, and very willing, but he did get easily distracted. He had been getting back later and later with each passing day from his round of deliveries. Merry, aware that Aunt Adelaide was just waiting for Robert to slip, had several times covered up for Robert's relaxed attitude to their deliveries.

On Friday, the big delivery van had arrived, driven by one of Sean's drivers, who explained that he had been ordered to take over the deliveries-- and at short notice, he added in an aggrieved tone.

Merry fumed. She tried to ring the hotel suite, but there was no answer. Where was Robert? Why hadn't he had the decency to contact her if he had decided not to work on Friday? She then remembered all the times that Robert was less than responsible, when he had offered to help in the past. Her ill temper grew.

"You know Robert," Aunt Adelaide said cautiously. "He might have decided to go away for the weekend."

"He would not have," Merry snapped, suspecting that it was certainly what he had done. "He knows how busy we are on Fridays!"

However, the day passed and there was no sign of him. Nor did he ring to apologize. Merry's temper worsened. Aunt Adelaide wore her 'I told you so' expression and remained silent.

Sean turned up in the late afternoon and Merry, through gritted teeth, thanked him for the loan of one of his drivers for the day.

"I've arranged for him to do the extra deliveries from now on," Sean said casually. "I noticed that working here was disrupting Robert's social life."

"You sacked him!" Merry cried, forgetting her own annoyance at Robert's irresponsibility in her fury at Sean's interference in something that was none of his business. "That's why he didn't turn up today!"

"I could hardly sack someone who wasn't employed," Sean pointed out. "He wouldn't have turned up anyway! He's gone sailing with Toni up the coast for a few days."

"You must have told him not to come back, anyway," she said. "You had no right to interfere with my staff arrangements. Robert worked very hard all this week at Merriland's."

"His public relations gestures were too expensive for either Merriland's or Westwood to afford," Sean said. "On Monday, he left a trail of red roses with the receptionists of all the city hotels. On Tuesday, he gave our floral arrangements to four elderly citizen homes. On Wednesday, those particularly expensive arrangements ordered for the opening of the new hotel arrived at the children's ward of the local hospital."

"And that's a reason for interfering with my arrangements," Merry blazed. She thought with regret of the hours of work she had put into the floral arrangements for the foyer of the hotel opening, and remembered that Robert never did live by other people's standards. She rallied herself and plunged into attack. "I consider that straight good public relations. You spend a fortune more on advertising. Think of the goodwill his gestures will bring!"

"Very expensive goodwill gestures," Sean admitted smoothly. "I told him not to bother to help out again." He paused. "I told him to go because he went to the races yesterday with Toni and seven hundred dollars collected on behalf of Westwoods."

"That doesn't make him dishonest," Merry protested. "You know that he will pay it back. It is only the equivalent of his wages anyway."

"And didn't finish the rest of the deliveries," Sean continued, ignoring Merry's interruption. "Three reception rooms and one wedding, and that was an exercise in public relations no business needs."

"It was still not your place to say anything," Merry flung back at Sean.

"I happen to be the senior partner in this organization, my girl, so I assure you I have the perfect right to protect our business interests. If you take it up with your father I'm sure you will find that he agrees."

Merry was silenced. She knew perfectly well that her father and Aunt Adelaide would agree with Sean. It was odd how everyone closed ranks in their united disapproval of Robert. No one ever praised or admired Robert for his generosity, willingness to help anyone, and his easy-going tolerance.

"This is a business we are running, not a charitable institution and like most businesses there are certain rules to follow to survive. Like being responsible and conscientious and not too light-fingered." He nodded to Aunt Adelaide and strolled out of the shop. Merry watched him leave in impotent fury.

Aunt Adelaide looked thoughtful. "I did tell you so," she said at last. "That Robert is a rogue. Your father is going to be very upset when he finds out what Robert has done this time."

Merry breathed hard. She was furious with Robert for letting her down so disgracefully, but for some reason the brunt of her fury was directed at the senior partner of Westwood and Merriland's.

She hated Sean Westwood, she fumed to herself. Robert was irresponsible and inclined to despise the acquisitive instincts of a material society, but he was generous, open-handed, and honest. Definitely honest, Merry reminded herself. She would make sure he returned that seven hundred dollars the very next time she saw him.

"How many more orders are there left to make up?" she managed in a tone of total unconcern, indicating to Aunt Adelaide that the matter of Robert was finished as a topic of conversation. But not forgotten, she vowed to herself, as she ruthlessly stripped leaves and twisted blossoms to shape.

Chapter 6

Robert, arriving at the shop a week later, tanned and relaxed from his week's sailing, was amused at the stir he had created. He peeled off the seven hundred dollars from a thick wad and shrugged away the disapproval of his Aunt Adelaide and Merry's bitter words about his irresponsible actions.

"Think of all the goodwill I engendered for Westwood and Merriland's," he had pointed out. "Known as good public relations, isn't it?"

Robert's gesture towards the hospital and the nursing home had attracted favourable publicity and extra custom, which Merry hadn't been slow to point out to the unimpressed Sean and her father. With the money safely back to balance the books Merry relented.

"Is this a social visit?"

"Of course!" Robert assured his favourite relatives. He examined their concerned expressions. "I'm not asking for the privilege of helping at the shop again, honest! Just wanted to know if the weekender is still with the Lands' family?"

Aunt Adelaide's face softened. The small cottage above the snowline belonged to her. She usually let it during the snow season, and in the summer the family often spent their weekends up there.

"The key is in its usual position under the third pot plant," she said, guessing the inevitable request. "And this time, Robert, please clean up before you leave."

Robert kissed his aunt and Merry and drove off. He was still driving the red Lamborghini. Merry wondered whether the volatile Toni was still in town, or had they had another of their frequent fights? Over the weeks Toni seemed to spend a lot of her time with Sean or waiting at his office. Robert had all the appearance of a man at a loose end.

It was just as they were finishing up on Saturday that Sean's secretary Jane Mollison rang. She sounded almost uncomfortable under her impersonal brisk friendliness. First, she wanted to know if Sean was there, or perhaps Tom Land. He had already left the nursery and she wanted to speak to him urgently. She then hesitated, and asked if Merry would mind dropping by on her way home.

"I'll leave the door unlocked," she promised. "There seems to be a slight problem."

Merry agreed to drop by. She was surprised to hear from Jane. The office staff didn't usually work on the weekend. Jane explained that she had to put in extra time getting the figures ready for the auditors' report.

"I know," Aunt Adelaide whispered as she eavesdropped. "I sent our figures in yesterday."

"Don't worry Dad about anything," Merry warned. "I don't suppose it's anything I can't handle."

She kissed her aunt and promised to see her back home later in the afternoon. The basement parking lot of Westwood's office building was closed. Merry found a parking spot in the front. She went up in the lift to the deserted suite of offices.

Jane looked tired but managed a smile at her arrival. She sat at her desk with neat piles of schedules, bank statements and invoice books around her.

"I came in today to double check the figures more discreetly," she explained. "I discovered some nasty discrepancies."

Merry sat down and studied the cheque stubs against the bank statements. "Where?" she asked in bewilderment.

Jane raised her eyebrows. She pointed from one set of figures to the other. After a while, Merry who was scribbling furiously on a scrap of paper, started to add up the miserable pattern of the extra payments. It amounted to forty-five thousand dollars! From the bank statements it looked as if altered cheque amounts had been presented. None of them matched up with the figures on the cheque stubs.

"Very clever," Merry said tonelessly.

All the altered cheques had been presented within the past month. Robert had been down in Melbourne for exactly five weeks! Merry's heart sank. She felt physically sick as she remembered the first family row when the youthful Robert had left home. He had forged his father's signature for six hundred dollars. He had evidently acquired more expensive tastes since then.

"Very neat!" Jane explained. "I double checked on the bank statements." Her finger pointed to the damning figures again. "The cheques were altered and presented through the suburban banks. There was no reason for them to be queried."

"No." Merry agreed dully, remembering her light-hearted assurance that the problem would be nothing that she couldn't handle.

Forty-five thousand dollars! And several cheques were drawn on the joint Westwood and Merrilands' account! What had Robert wanted so much money for? What had possessed him to do such a dreadful thing? There must be a reasonable explanation for it! Robert was irresponsible and careless, but he couldn't be a thief! She thought of Sean's barely concealed dislike of Robert, and the office seemed to close in on her. Sean would believe the worst of Robert! He wouldn't think twice about sending him to jail!

"What?" she exclaimed.

Jane was still talking. "I said it must be an insider--someone who was able to have access to back invoices to copy and present the company with the changed addresses. All for smallish amounts that wouldn't be queried, and then the cheque figures altered."

"What addresses?" Merry asked, picking up the pile of invoices and looking at them.

Robert was often in the office with Toni, collecting her or waiting for her, and leaning over desks flirting with the office staff.

"Post office box numbers," Jane explained. "A phony name and address and uncheckable!"

"Where's Sean?" Merry asked.

She looked again at the damning figures on her scrap of paper. She was thinking fast. If she could catch up with Robert and get him to come back and somehow fix things up before the auditors arrived on the Monday, surely everything could be smoothed over. There just had to be a logical explanation for what he had done! Robert was many things, but she didn't believe he was a thief.

"I don't know," Jane confessed. "He had a phone call late yesterday and rushed off. I think he might have gone interstate for a few days."

"Let me discuss it with Dad and Aunt Adelaide," Merry suggested. "I've got a copy of the figures here. I can probably catch up with Sean on Sunday evening and see what he wants to do."

"He'll have to know before the auditors arrive on Monday," Jane agreed. She looked relieved as she started to pack everything away in the safe. "It was just that I wanted to be very careful and discreet. It looks like an inside job, but there's no action we can take before Sean makes some decision."

"Of course," Merry agreed, as she clenched her hands into fists and tried to control the tremor in her voice.

She watched Jane lock the safe, and they left the building together. Once alone, Merry thought about what to do. Robert must have gone to the cottage for the weekend. In her small car it was a four-hour drive up there. For the first time in her life Merry wished she lived apart from her over- anxious, careful father and aunt. She had to think up an excuse to get away that wouldn't arouse their suspicions.

At the service station, as she was filling the petrol tank, she had a sudden inspiration! She was smiling in relief as she dialled home.

"Aunt Adelaide, Sean asked me to inspect that new reception place up in the hills. You know, the one we have to supply the flowers for next week."

"Oh, dear! You won't be home for hours then," her aunt grumbled.

"So don't wait up," Merry returned. "And make sure Dad doesn't worry."

It was a long drive in the small car. Merry had plenty of time to worry about everything. She drove steadily through the sprawling outer suburbs. She had a copy of the dates as well as the amounts stolen. Could she match it to Robert's movements at all, to puzzle out the reason?

The land opened out into the flat grazing country. Soon the sharp blue mass of the mountains appeared. The temperature dropped, and mist appeared, softening the hollows of the gullies. Merry stopped the car and changed into her comfortable working clothes: frayed runners, heavy jeans, and her raggy dark jumper. She should have gone home and changed into warmer clothes, but that would have entailed questions, and she desperately had to speak to Robert alone.

Alone! She suddenly remembered. There was no likelihood that Robert would be alone! He probably went up to the cottage for the weekend with

Toni! She could hardly discuss the delicate matter of him stealing from the company in front of Toni! How was she to going to drag him away from the possessive Toni long enough to discuss anything?

She turned the problem over and over in her mind as she drove. The countryside was changing, the land tilting into the foothills and the trees thickened into dense bushland. After a while she stopped worrying and concentrated on her driving. The sun had dropped behind the mountains and it was suddenly dark. The thick mist rose from the gullies to encroach on the road and the Mini skidded on wet patches when she took the curves too fast.

At last she turned into the old timber cutters' road, which cut across the valley and then back on to the metalled road up the steep mountainside to Aunt Adelaide's cottage. The darkness of the bush closed against the narrowing track. Merry slowed down as the Mini ploughed its way through the deep ruts and puddles. Several times she had to squeeze past healthy young saplings, growing arrogantly down the centre of the track.

She tried to remember when she had last used the short cut. Could those saplings have grown so high in eighteen months? Obviously the track wasn't used very frequently. She bit her lip as she scraped the Mini between two trees barring her way. They had no right to be so well established. She was already regretting using the short cut.

The metalled road was an hour longer, but it would have been safer. If she broke down here, no one was going to be able to find her to come to her assistance! She slowed to drive more carefully, peering through the blackness and weaving past the trees that now crowded the track. The further along she drove, the higher and more thickly clustered the trees became, until the track was only guessed at by the ancient wheel ruts.

She stopped the car. Was she better off going back to the highway? She glanced back at the blackness and sighed. There was no room to turn the Mini, and she couldn't weave in reverse all the way back to the turn-off. The track sloped downward. Only a short space ahead should be the log bridge over the creek. A short haul up the hill would have her back on the metalled road. She was nearly through! She glanced at her watch. It had taken her six hours to get this far. This route no longer came under the heading of a short cut.

She kept on with her cautious weaving between the trees. When she reached the creek, the yellow beam of the headlights showed only a single log across the creek! The heavy sleepers and the solid tree trunks of the small bridge were broken and scattered along the gully like a child's toy. Merry frowned as she remembered the previous winter of floods. She knew that they had been severe, but the bridge had lasted eighty years of floods.

She tried to remember the network of tracks that criss-crossed the gully. There should be a shallow ford further down the hill, if the disused track hadn't become too overgrown. She nudged the Mini between two tree ferns and bumped her way slowly through the darkness. The track should intersect just down the hill. However, the track seemed to have vanished. Still, apart from being very steep, the ground was fairly open.

Once she had to edge around a fallen tree, crackling and rustling as she drove over the riotous undergrowth until she picked up the relative clearness of the disused track. At last she reached the creek. She stopped the car and examined the water. It swirled over what seemed a shallow rocky base. She was going to have to risk it. She drove across, and up the other side.

The bushland seemed less encroaching on this side of the creek. She changed into a lower gear and battled up a definite track. She had nearly reached the turn-off to the metalled road and had relaxed her vigilance for a split second. The Mini tilted awkwardly into a deeper rut than usual and there was a loud crack. The wheel grated and shuddered its protest and stopped turning. Merry turned the engine off.

Her Mini had gone as far as it could. She had to face the fact that she wasn't going to be able to drive it anywhere tonight. Perhaps Robert could tow it out in the morning and maybe see what the damage was. She was going to have to walk the rest of the distance. Fortunately, the metalled road was close enough. She started the long trudge up the steep winding hill to the cottage. She kept turning hopefully, but the road remained dark and silent. It started to drizzle and became steadily colder. She put her hands in her pockets. Her runners sloshed through the run-off water by the side of the road.

She was chilled, wet and hungry by the time she reached the turn-off to the small cottage. Her heart sank as she came up the winding drive. The cottage was in darkness! Robert hadn't arrived yet! She found the key under the third pot plant and opened up.

The smell of the house hit her, a dusty smell intertwined with the overpowering woodsmoke, a combination of odours that brought back vivid memories of their weekends of roaring open fires and the toast they used to make in front of it. She turned on the light. The friendly sitting room with its shabby couches and crowded untidy bookshelves greeted her. She saw that the big fireplace was already set. The matches were in their usual place on the mantelpiece. She lit the fire. There were pinecones among the wood and paper, and the fire roared and crackled into healthy life.

Merry stood admiring the way it was burning before rousing herself. She realized that she was icy cold and her clothes were saturated. She went through the wardrobes but could only find an old dressing gown to wear. She stripped off her wet clothes and put it on. It might have been an old one of Robert's, as it seemed too large to have belonged to her father.

She went back to the sitting room and draped her wet clothes on the hearth guard, watching as the steam started to rise from them. The fire threw out a lot of heat, crackling and spitting with cheerful efficiency.

She filled the kettle and put it on the hob. There was a store of tinned goods and tinned milk in the kitchen cupboard and a cache of flour, but no bread. After she had a hot cup of tea, she would make some griddle scones she decided, although Robert would probably bring supplies with him.

She sat down and relaxed, stretching out her bare feet to the warmth of the fire. There was nothing she could do tonight and her mobile was out of range up here. In the morning, she and Robert could tow the Mini out and down to the nearest garage, and he could drop her back home.

With luck she would be back before anyone realized that she had been missing all night. It was fortunate, she thought as she stretched more comfortably on the couch, that Aunt Adelaide never disturbed her on Sunday mornings. They wouldn't worry about her non-appearance before lunchtime. She stoked up the fire with some of the heavier wood and settled to watching the kettle boil.

She became warmer and then sleepy. Her thoughts started to drift back over all the holidays she had spent at the cottage. This corner of the couch had always been her favourite spot to read or to dream away the long evenings. There was an unchanging feel to the cottage, as though time stood still. Perhaps it had something to do with the fact that Aunt Adelaide never redecorated. If she repainted, it was always in the original colours of brown and stone.

Suddenly, there was a loud knock on the door, waking her out of her doze. The kettle was hissing and splattering droplets of steam on the fire. She scrambled to her feet, pulling the dressing gown more tightly around her and rushed to open the door, light-hearted with relief. Robert had arrived at last!

"Thank goodness, Robert," she greeted the tall shadow at the door. "I've been waiting hours and hours for you."

"Really," drawled a familiar voice. "So, we will be able to wait together, won't we?"

It was Sean Westwood! He walked into the room and turned to face her. She shut the door on the cold gust of wind that came in with him. The room was warm and cozy in the flickering firelight, but a chill spread through her at the tight fury of his face.

The embezzled forty-five thousand dollars was obviously no longer a secret!

Chapter 7

"Where is he?" Sean demanded.

He wore a heavy jumper over casual slacks and paced up and down the room, as if it was impossible for him to stand still. The normally good humoured expression was missing from his face.

"He's not here," Merry answered.

Sean searched the small cottage. First, he checked the two bedrooms and built-in back veranda. His footsteps echoed hollowly as he checked the laundry, bathroom and then the kitchen.

Merry leaned closer to the warmth of the fire and waited. Why had he come up here? Had Aunt Adelaide told him that Robert was going to use the weekend cottage? If Sean had been talking to her, he would know that Merry was supposed to be checking out the hills' reception place on his instructions! Was he going to ask questions about that, too?

She shivered and huddled closer to the fire. She was chilled by the furious expression on his face when he came back into the room. This was not a man who could discuss the problem of the forty-five thousand embezzled dollars in a reasonable manner! For whatever reason Robert had done such a dreadful thing, she had to protect him until Sean settled down.

"Where's your car?" he demanded.

"I broke an axle or something on the old timber cutters' road," she explained. She wrapped the dressing gown around her more tightly. "Would you like a cup of tea?"

"Perhaps Robert dropped you here and went out for supplies?" he suggested. "There seems to be quite a few discrepancies not only in the books, but in your expected movements." His eyes inspected the dressing gown and her bare feet beneath. "I can see that this close friendship with your cousin Robert is very convenient."

Merry flushed in temper.

"Such very close kissing cousins," he mocked. "Close enough to cold-bloodedly cheat your own family to help Robert! I should admire a man who can keep Toni under control and still have your loyalty, the company money, and whatever else you bestow on him."

"How dare you!" Merry raged.

"How dare I!" he exclaimed. "How dare I indeed! Forty-five thousand dollars short on the books and the delivery van is missing as well! So is Robert! And you are conveniently waiting for him in such an isolated place."

"It doesn't happen to be any business of yours," Merry flung back, forgetting her earlier resolution to handle him tactfully. "Did you ever get taught to mind your own business? Did you go to see my father just to snoop on my movements?"

"As your father and aunt seemed to think I was responsible for sending you off on company business in the hills, I should imagine it is very much my business," he returned.

"So!" Merry seethed. She felt a pulse beating in her temples, and she seemed to be having trouble breathing evenly. "I am now an accredited thief, liar and accomplice. Why not a potential home wrecker--am I supposed to have come between Robert and Toni as well?"

"You are a little fool," he said. "Toni was the one who suggested I should look to what you and Robert were doing! She certainly wasn't with Robert."

"Well, he isn't with me." The rage that made Merry shake so much, and stopped her from thinking why she felt so hurt and wounded took over. She flung herself at him.

He caught her flailing arms and held her still. She flung her head back to get her hair out of her eyes and glared at him, ignoring the fact that the dressing gown had slipped from her shoulders.

He stared at her in consternation. She held his gaze for what seemed a lifetime. His grey eyes actually had gold flecks radiating out from the compelling enlarged black pupils. Her breath came in sobbing gasps. Her pulse slowed its beat in her throat. The moment tightened until it hurt. He suddenly released her. There was horror on his face.

"I'm sorry - I didn't mean..."

Merry's rage evaporated. He looked vulnerable and shocked and not at all like his good humoured and so very in control self.

He picked up her arms again very gently. He bent his head and kissed her hands lightly. "I didn't mean to grab you," he apologized again.

Merry stared at his bowed head. He had come raging into the hut, jumped to a wrong conclusion and enraged her to the stage she wanted to claw his eyes out or else burst into tears. Then he had apologized!

"Oh, Merry love," he groaned suddenly. "Why does it have to be like this?"

To her complete bewilderment he pulled her against him, lowered his head, and gently touched her lips with his mouth. Her mouth had dropped open, at first in astonishment, and then to her shame, it clung to his mouth as though some force was impelling it to soften under the warm mouth over it. His kiss became more demanding and urgent.

Tremors of weakness swept over her. She felt simultaneously both detached and involved. It was as if this was happening to a third person, a tempestuous alien young girl with lashes sweeping over pink cheeks, leaning against the tall man as though enchanted. The stranger pulled tightly against her with a reckless abandon.

Yet she was that girl, alive and aware in every nerve ending, from her tangled hair tickling down her bare back, to the prickly coir matting under her bare toes. She felt desire surge through her with every pulse beat, aware of everything but imprisoned in a moment that stretched for an eternity. Nothing was important but the warm mouth parting hers; the rough knit of his jumper against her bare skin as her shaking body tried to mould itself against him.

"Oh, Merry," he whispered. "How could you do this to me?"

He picked her up and carried her over to the couch. Merry's eyes were large and questioning. The dressing gown had fallen away from her body, but she ignored it as suddenly unimportant. She stretched out her arms to him in an unconscious appeal.

He stared at her for a moment, almost bemused and shook his head. Suddenly he turned his back on her and walked over to speak to the closed door leading to the kitchen.

"If your clothes are dry, why don't you get dressed?" he suggested calmly. "I saw some tinned soup in the kitchen. I'll heat it up."

He opened the door and vanished through, shutting it after him. Merry heard the clattering of kitchen utensils. She stared at the closed door in bewilderment. Why had he pulled away from her like that? It seemed almost in revulsion! What had caused his sudden change of mood?

Sanity returned with a shocking rush. The warmth and dreamy languor vanished. Merry spared an incredulous look at herself. She was draped like a half-naked rag doll across the couch! She shook her head in disbelief and jumped to her feet.

As she pulled on her underwear, dry jeans and jumper, the embarrassment spread. Her cheeks were fiery with her blushes, and she felt sticky all over. She had nearly let herself be carried away! If Sean hadn't been the one who stopped the kissing, the strange abandoned Merry in hiding under her reserved exterior was quite prepared to surrender rapturously to the man who was her bitterest enemy! *How could she forget her wary reserve so easily?* She berated herself. But the stranger who had responded so instantly and passionately to that kiss appeared to have gone, so the bewildering question remained unanswered.

By the time Sean had returned with two steaming mugs of hot soup, she had herself under control, and thinking fast. If Robert was not with Toni, he and the missing van were quite likely to turn up at the cottage. She remembered that Robert often used to say that the cottage was a good retreat to think out problems. Therefore, she had to get Sean away from the cottage as quickly as possible.

She met his eyes steadily as he handed over the mug. She felt more in control now that she was dressed. There was nothing at all feminine or suggestive about her garb now. The heavy dark jumper fell shapelessly down over her work-stained old jeans. She was dressed like any other early morning worker in the industry. She sprawled her feet, in their securely laced sneakers, across the warmth of the hearth and opened her attack.

"You're wasting your time staying here. Robert has probably gone interstate."

"So, we'll waste time," he agreed. He sounded resigned rather than annoyed.

The couch creaked as he sat down beside her and stretched his feet out as well. Merry repressed an impulse to laugh hysterically. The pair of them must look like a staid married couple, sitting side by side in front of the open fire. Then she met his gaze. The impulse to laugh vanished. She studied her hot tomato soup.

"Aunt Adelaide will be worried if I'm not back soon."

"You can't be expected to go too far with a broken axle," he returned.

Merry sneaked a look at him. He looked completely in control of both himself and the situation. Merry sipped at the hot soup and tried to work out what to do. She became aware of the heavy rain drumming down on the tin roof.

"You could take me home," she suggested. "Dad is going to get worried if I don't get back tonight."

"As soon as I have had a little talk with Robert."

"And I tell you, he's not coming up here," Merry insisted.

"So you keep saying," he replied.

Merry finished the soup and stood up. "Well, I'm not staying," she retorted. "I'll start walking back right now."

Sean reached up and pulled her down beside him again. "And perhaps meet Robert on his way up? We'll stay here until he arrives."

"Dad will be dreadfully worried," she insisted.

"They probably won't notice your absence until tomorrow," he guessed. "We'll be back by then."

"Jane said she thought that you had gone away unexpectedly Friday night," Merry probed. His nearness was making her treacherous pulse thud again.

"A hysterical call from my aunt because they had this big drama with Toni," he explained with a sigh. "I drove up and found Toni had stormed off."

"You found her?"

Sean had said that Toni was the one who had accused Robert. Had Toni been suspicious when Robert had turned up with unexplained money? Had she been so upset that she had gone off and left him?

"I hired a plane in the morning. One of her friends owns an island and she went to earth there." Sean's voice was dry. "She then admitted that she and Robert were through and that he had taken the money. After I got back, I drove down, checked the books and visited your father. I discovered Robert had asked to use the cottage and you had lied about your movements."

"So you kept on driving up here," Merry said. "You are wasting your time and your petrol. I came up here on impulse."

"Without even buying some bread and milk?"

The silence between them lengthened. The rain drummed down on the roof. Merry gazed into the glowing heart of the fire. For a while she sat tensely, listening for the distinctive sound of wheels on the gravel of the drive.

Where would Robert have gone if he wasn't coming up to the cottage? Why had he taken the money in the first place? He always said he preferred his independence to money. If he ever made his peace with his parents, they would give him anything he asked for. He didn't have to steal.

She relaxed and yawned. She was very tired and the heat was making her drowsy. Soon she was dreaming. She sat beside Robert on the high front bench of the van. He was driving over open sea. She was pleading with him to return and Robert was laughing at her. He wouldn't take her seriously! After a while she gave up her arguments and enjoyed the ride. She became aware of the vast expanse of peaceful and empty ocean they were driving through. She felt very relaxed as she listened to the water splashing and gurgling around them.

She opened her eyes. She still felt very relaxed and comfortable. She was tucked up in one of the beds in the spare bedroom, the daylight dim and grey through the ceaseless cascade of water against the window. The gurgling was the familiar sound of the rainwater filling the water tank by the window.

The misery returned with her memory of the previous evening. Sean must have put her to bed! Had Robert arrived during the evening? She climbed out of bed, noticing that her heavy jumper and sneakers were on the floor beside her.

She sniffed. The smell of hot porridge was in the air! She slipped on her jumper, laced up her shoes, then opened the kitchen door quietly. Sean stirred a pot over the small electric stove. He glanced down at her. It wasn't an unfriendly look.

"You can have porridge with honey, and stale coffee and condensed milk," he said briskly. "Otherwise, your aunt's cupboards are bare."

"Did Robert arrive?"

"No."

"Told you so," Merry said, trying to keep the relief out of her voice. "Can you drop me down at the local garage, so I can get them to tow the Mini out?"

"It should be on its way," he explained. "I went down there first thing this morning. They are fitting another kingpin for you. It should be ready about noon. Couldn't buy any bread or milk though."

"The local store doesn't open on Sunday," Merry said. She glanced at her watch. The greyness of the light was due to the heavy rain, not early morning.

It was already ten o'clock! "If this weather keeps on, the road through the valley could be flooded."

She sniffed at the porridge and realized she wasn't hungry. She was starving! All she had to eat the previous night was the mug of soup. She set the table with tablecloth and crockery and sneaked another look at Sean. His hair was ruffled and his face unshaven. His face seemed younger as he concentrated on stirring the porridge.

"Do you believe me when I said Robert wasn't coming up?" she asked.

"No," he said. "I think he saw my car and kept on going. I should have put my car around the back. I fear I have scared off our light-fingered Robert."

The cottage suddenly stopped being cozy and homelike. The silence lasted as they ate their porridge, drowned in evaporated milk and honey and drank their coffee. Merry tidied up the kitchen and Sean cleaned out and reset the fire.

She shut and locked the front door and replaced the key in its hiding place. Sean opened up the door of the Mercedes for her and got in himself. It was an hour drive down to the garage and it rained relentlessly all the way down, the gullies at the sides of the road swollen with the rushing water.

The cheerful mechanic had retrieved and fixed up the Mini. Merry could only guess what sort of money or promises Sean had made to get him to fix it on the Sunday. He waved her off and slammed down the garage door. Sean spoke at last as she got into her car.

"I'll follow you back to make sure everything is all right," he said. He paused and then added. "There won't be any publicity over the missing money. I'll adjust the matter before the auditors do the books."

"That's generous of you," Merry said through stiff lips.

"I shall consider it a personal matter between Robert and myself," he continued. He gestured for her to drive off.

The Mini started cheerfully. She turned on the windscreen wipers as she drove through the blinding rain. The Mercedes followed behind all the wearisome way back. Merry thought about Sean's statement. There wouldn't be a public exposure of Robert's theft! It was very decent of him, she admitted to herself. Also he had driven the long distance down to arrange to have her car fixed.

Then she remembered the implied threat that he would consider it a personal matter. She shivered and turned her heater up. Robert was temporarily reprieved from disaster! She should be feeling relieved, but for some reason she had to restrain an irrational impulse to tears. Her mind went around in miserable circles all the tiring and depressing drive back to her home. Although Sean was going to take steps to stop any scandal or publicity, he had obviously decided that Robert's disappearance was proof of his guilt.

Eventually, Merry's misery and self-searching crystallized into a definite decision. She was going to have to find Robert herself and discover what really had happened!

Chapter 8

The grey Mercedes veered off in the heavy rain. Merry turned her car into her driveway and stopped the car.

She sat for a few minutes. It was later than she had planned on arriving home on Sunday morning. There was no way she could sneak into the house and pretend that she had been home all night! She took a deep breath and went into the house.

Her father and Aunt Adelaide were in the cozy living room. Her father was immersed in a book on orchid culture, and Aunt Adelaide was setting up the tea tray. They looked up as she came in. Merry braced herself for the inevitable scolding, but they seemed remarkably unconcerned.

"Hello, Merry," her father greeted her. "Had a nice trip?"

"Just in time for a cup of tea," Aunt Adelaide said, as she reached for another cup. "Everything all right?"

"Sure," Merry agreed.

Of course it wasn't all right! Merry studied them cautiously. She hadn't been home all night, yet there were no questions, and no worried faces. Where did they think she had been?

"You weren't worried about me not getting back last night?" she ventured at last.

"Sean said not to worry," Aunt Adelaide explained. "He intended to collect you on his way through. He wasn't really happy about you taking the Mini all the way up to the Vistaview Receptions."

"Thoughtful of him," Merry ground out,

"When he said that you were both going on afterwards to the cottage to see Robert, I suggested it would be better to stay overnight instead of driving straight back," Aunt Adelaide continued. "It's a nasty drive down the mountains after dark when the weather breaks."

Merry drank her tea in silence. Her father obviously hadn't been told about the forged cheques. She stopped drinking. Another more dreadful thought occurred to her. Surely Sean wouldn't have suspected that her father and aunt were involved as well? When he had arrived at the cottage, he had seemed very certain that she had been Robert's accomplice!

Was he trying to lull her father and Aunt Adelaide into a false sense of security by remaining silent about everything? She tried to work out his movements since the moment when Toni would have accused Robert. Once he had driven back, discovered the van was missing, and examined the damning evidence of the forged cheques the next logical step would have been to check out the other partners. But he hadn't told them anything!

Once her father had mentioned her reason for going up to the cottage, his suspicions about her involvement would have been confirmed, especially as Aunt Adelaide had told him that Robert was probably at the weekend cottage. He couldn't have aroused their suspicions at all that anything was wrong! He must have just smoothly reassured them as to her movements, and then driven straight up.

"I'm glad you weren't worried," she said lamely.

"Sean is very sensible," Aunt Adelaide said with a smile. "I never worry about you when he is around."

Merry remembered the fury on Sean's face the previous night and shivered. She thought about Robert and the implied threat of Sean's retaliation for his actions and shivered again. She didn't share her aunt's misplaced confidence in him. Despite his air of good humour Sean would be a dangerous man to cross.

"Have another cup of tea," Aunt Adelaide ordered. "You must be chilled right through. That cold front looks like its settling in for a spell."

It did settle in, and the next week was made unpleasant with the sleeting rain and the cold. Flower arrangements seemed to survive longer, and Merry spent less time creating and replacing them. Apart from the weddings already booked, and the constant replacements of the established flower arrangements, there were long periods when Merry had very little to do. What Aunt Adelaide called 'the romantic impulse' buying had dropped right away.

"Bad weather for romance," Aunt Adelaide grumbled, as she brewed herself another pot of tea. "A young man's fancy must only turn to love and roses when the temperature rises." She glanced sharply at Merry, who hadn't thought this witticism funny enough to laugh at, "You sickening for something, child? You seem very peaky this week."

"Bored with not enough work to keep busy," Merry explained.

Although it wasn't boredom, it was the heavy inexplicable depression hanging over her. There was still no sign of Robert, or any word from him. He and the van seemed to have vanished completely. As the slow, grey days passed, she became more and more convinced that he really was guilty.

She was relieved that he wasn't going to have to go to jail, but the depression seemed to be compounded of her disappointment with Robert and somehow Sean's attitude. Sean was brisk, cheerful and businesslike every time he came through the shop, but her depression settled more deeply after each of his visits.

For some reason, the thought that he really believed that she could stoop to helping Robert steal upset her. Not, she told herself, that she really cared what he thought about her! But the wound festered. Why was he so quick to doubt her honesty and integrity just over the coincidence of her looking for Robert?

"You definitely do look peaky," Aunt Adelaide mused one afternoon. "Why don't you go and work at the Arcade shop for a few days? It's very bright up there. They get all the lunch hour office trade and they are always busy."

Merry stared at her in horror. It was the main Westwood shop. Sean was in and out of it all day. "I'd hate to work there," she snapped. "It would be like working on a factory conveyor belt! None of the work is individual or very special and personal."

"Why don't you go up to the nursery and help your Dad for a few days," Aunt Adelaide suggested.

Merry was almost tempted. The new orchid nursery was a fascinating place to work, but then she remembered. Sean also spent all the afternoons he could get away up there with her father. Their joint obsession with the orchids had drawn them very close together. She would only be the odd man out if she went up there.

"Dad doesn't need me up there," she pointed out.

"Why don't you hole up in the cottage for a few days?" Aunt Adelaide tried again.

"Never!" Merry exclaimed. Her mind flinched away from her rapturous response to Sean's kiss, and his horrid assumption of her guilt. From now on the cottage held unbearably painful memories.

Aunt Adelaide rattled the mugs in the little sink with a grim look on her face. "That settles it," she snapped. "You are definitely going to take a few days off, or I will march you straight around to old Doctor Ingle for a check-up. You must be sickening for something."

"Don't be silly, Aunt Adelaide." Merry hastened to placate her worried aunt. "It's just this dreary weather."

Her aunt remained silent. That night, her father also looked thoughtful. He studied her carefully as she sat down for dinner. She caught the look in his eyes and wrinkled her nose.

"A penny for them, Dad," she demanded.

"A two dollar coin would be more to the point," he returned. "You do look a bit peaky, my girl. What about going away for a few days--everything is slack enough with this cold front."

"Go where?" Merry asked with a shrug. "Weather is weather wherever you go."

"Just been talking to Marilyn," he said. "She'd love to see you. A few days along the coast will make a change. Watch all the storms come over."

Merry opened her mouth to protest her dislike of staying with her aunt and Uncle. They had a large house down on the peninsula. Her uncle travelled a lot, over-seeing his business interests, and her aunt went to, and gave endless cocktail and dinner parties.

Her refusal was slowed by a sudden thought. What if Robert's parents had seen him lately? She knew that he didn't have any time for his parents. 'That sour faced couple who call themselves my parents,' he had always sneered. Still, he had officially become engaged. Surely, he would have contacted his parents, even taken Toni to meet them?

Merry sighed in relief. She could do something positive about her depression and uncertainty about Robert. If she went to stay with her aunt and uncle, she might be able to discover some clue to Robert's present whereabouts. If only she could find him and get him to explain just exactly what he wanted the forty-five thousand dollars for. It was such an awkward amount! Not enough to buy a business or a house, or even a boat! Perhaps he had wanted it to buy Toni a ring? And what about the fight they must have had? Had Tony really broken her engagement over Robert's theft?

"Marilyn is always asking why you don't visit more often," her father was saying. "You know that you are the only niece she has, and Bill always says he likes to have you around."

"Don't hassle," Merry said meekly. "I'll go first thing in the morning, if Aunt Adelaide can manage alone."

"Well, I can," was the reply. "But Sean can always send over some help from the other shop if I get into trouble. You go and do some socializing down at Winterview."

Merry wrinkled her nose at that. She was fond enough of her other aunt, but a few days of her company would be enough. She was a very social person and liked to get through life with a minimum of discomfort, although she always meant well.

The next day, Merry drove along the beach road in the pouring rain. The grey flatness of the bay was closed in by the heavier grey of the rain squalls as they moved inland, and her windscreen wipers laboured to cope with the water.

Despite the greyness of the bay and the wet slickness of the roads, Merry was almost cheerful for the first time in days. She normally didn't have that much contact with Robert's parents. She resented the way her father was patronized as the poor relation of the family. As she grew older, she realized that her aunt and uncle were the ones to be pitied. What use was it having all that money and no love in the house?

Not that it was completely their fault, she mused as she turned off the beach road, and the Mini laboured up the steep slope of the mountain road. Robert was so very intolerant, as was his father, Bill Townsend. It must have been hard for them to cope with his complete rejection of their material society when he went through his alternative lifestyle stage. They were a rigid couple with set ideas and lacked any tolerance to cope with Robert during his difficult periods.

Her own tolerance was called into immediate use when she arrived at Winterview. It was just on noon. Her aunt and uncle came out to greet her as she drove the Mini under the elaborate porch shelter. She was picked up and kissed soundly by her uncle, his hard face softening with pleasure. She was then given a soft cheek to kiss by her aunt. The first attack was on her Mini.

"You know, you have a birthday coming up," her uncle reminded her. "What say I buy you a nice little red sports car instead of that dangerous heap?"

This had always been a familiar irritant to Merry. They found it easy to shower her with expensive presents, and Merry had been refusing them tactfully since her twelfth birthday. She made herself laugh in amusement, as she inspected her shabby Mini, the poor relation between the grey Bentley and the silver BMW.

"Now, Uncle Bill," she teased, "I love my Mini. Admit it's just sheer snobbery that you don't like my humble little heap of junk lowering the tone of your beautiful courtyard?"

It was the right way to handle the embarrassing offer. Her uncle's face cleared, and he gave a genuine laugh, and patted her on the shoulder. "You are a wretch, young Merry. I wish you would come and visit more often. Tom had no right to refuse to let Marilyn and I adopt you after Denise died. We wanted a daughter so badly."

"Maybe you will have to settle for a daughter-in-law and then a tribe of granddaughters." Merry turned the still painful subject skilfully. "Robert introduced a nice girl as his fiancée last time I saw him. Did he bring her here to meet you?"

Robert's parents exchanged a quick look. Her uncle looked thoughtful, and her aunt suddenly unhappy. Merry wondered if she had imagined their expressions.

"Toni Gamberton," her uncle agreed, a shade too heartily. "A very suitable match, and we are really thrilled about the fact that Robert at last is going to settle down."

"Such a nice girl," her aunt agreed mournfully.

Why so unhappy? Merry wondered, keeping the receptive smile on her face.

Her aunt cheered up almost immediately. "I hope you have brought down some nice clothes, because we want to show off our favourite niece while you are here."

"Not that it matters." her uncle assured her, as he collected her cases, wincing as he inspected the torn interior of the Mini. "Marilyn can buy you whatever you need. Come on up, your room is all ready for you."

As it always was, Merry thought as she looked around the beautiful room. Ever since she was a child, the room was always kept ready and waiting. Robert's parents could never understand that she preferred her own shabby home with Tom and Adelaide after the dreadful death of her mother and to struggle and work to help run the business, rather than choose a life of ease and luxury as their adopted daughter. Any more than they could understand why Robert preferred the tolerant home of his uncle and aunt, to the magnificent mansion on the side of the mountain overlooking the bay.

She sighed and unpacked her case. One of the disadvantages about visiting here was the assumption that she liked dressing up all the time. She was going to have to get changed into something more suitable immediately for their luncheon. She hadn't missed her aunt's horrified expression as she had scrambled out of the Mini in her shabby and comfortable working clothes.

She changed into her severely cut blue wool frock and pinned her hair up into a chignon. She refreshed her make-up and slipped into her high heels. The sophisticated, well-groomed reflection assured her she would pass muster. She went back downstairs into the big entertaining room.

She was quite sure that her aunt knew something. Her visit wasn't going to be wasted! That hint of unhappiness in aunt's eyes when she had mentioned Robert proved it. She was going to have to try to get her by herself for a confidential little talk and find out what they both were hiding.

The trouble with her aunt was that she disliked her own company and was never alone. Still, Merry would catch her by herself sooner or later. It was just a matter of patience. She was so engrossed in her thoughts that she had walked into the large room before she was aware that, as usual, her aunt and uncle were entertaining guests.

The murmur of voices died away. Everything was very quiet, almost too quiet, her instinct warned. She curved her mouth into a smile and looked towards the three people holding glasses by the wall of window. Her smile wobbled slightly.

Toni Gamberton, and her mother and father stared back in equal surprise. Toni's eyes started to get a dangerous glitter to them. Her parents just looked surprised as they recognized her.

"And this is our little niece Marilyn Land," her uncle introduced proudly. "Merry, I think you said you've already met Robert's fiancée Toni and of course I want you to meet her parents Mr. and Mrs. Gamberton."

"Of course we know Merry," Mrs. Gamberton gushed. Today her eyes were a lot friendlier, and her smile was wide, showing the perfect and well cared for teeth. "We are very happy to meet Sean's fiancée under such happy circumstances. Is Sean coming down for the weekend, too, my dear?'

Merry glared at Toni. She had almost forgotten that the quick-witted Toni had involved her in the phony engagement to Sean to make her own engagement to Robert more acceptable to her parents.

She sneaked a quick look at her aunt and uncle. They had almost stupefied expressions on their faces as the information penetrated. *Now the fat was really in the fire!* Merry thought frantically. *What was she supposed to do now?*

So, Toni thought it was funny to tangle her into this mess because she wanted to get her parents off her back about marrying Sean? Well, this mess was ending right now. She stared into Toni's suddenly imploring eyes and realized that Toni didn't think it was funny at all.

Chapter 9

"Engaged!" her aunt echoed blankly. "Tom never said a word about it!"

"Engaged, *hmm*," said her uncle. "When did this happen, Merry?"

"Of course Sean did say it was supposed to be kept quiet for a while," Mrs. Gamberton said with a laugh.

"Useful, though," agreed Mr. Gamberton in his satisfied way. "What with the business merging!"

"Very useful," agreed Merry's uncle. He smiled at Merry. "I'm glad to know you have got such a good head on your shoulders these days, my love. What does old Tom think about it all?"

"Dad doesn't know," Merry said with perfect truth. "Sean said it was to be kept quiet. He won't be down anyway." She snatched the excuse thankfully from the back of her mind. "The auditors are in--he's very busy."

"I bet old Tom is going to have to be talked around," her uncle said shrewdly. "He never did know what was good for you. Well, he won't hear about it from us."

"It's supposed to be a secret," Toni warned. There was a malicious sparkle in her black eyes. "Sean will be furious everyone knows."

And how! Merry thought ruefully. She turned the conversation by asking her uncle about when his auditors were due. He grumbled about their delay and this in turn brought in the trouble Mr. Gamberton had, managing to get his figures together for his end of year audit. This topic of conversation lasted until they had finished eating. Her uncle then turned the conversation back to Sean Westwood.

"He's got a good head on his shoulders," he decided. "You could do worse, you know, young Merry."

"Well, here's to the new fiancées," Toni's father said with a pleased smile, toasting Merry and Toni with his port. "I must say I am very happy that your Robert is part of such a good family."

Merry smiled but remained silent. She felt uncomfortable. Toni dimpled at her father as if she hadn't a care in the world. It seemed a very happy family gathering, except that Merry wasn't engaged to Sean, Robert was missing, and Toni had denounced him for stealing!

She recognized the pretty half hoop of diamonds Toni was wearing. Her grandmother had given it to Robert's mother. Robert must have been really serious about Toni if he had given her a family heirloom for an engagement ring! Did she consider herself still engaged to Robert after what he had done?

The afternoon dragged on and the rain sleeted down outside, so the open fire blazing in the big hearth made the room seem friendly and cozy. The music was an unnoticed accompaniment to their conversation. Merry handed around coffee and waited for her chance to speak to Toni alone.

At last Toni excused herself to freshen up her make-up. Merry followed her into the small bathroom and shut the door behind them. For a few seconds Merry studied Toni as she applied another coating of lipstick and patted her glossy black hair into neatness. Once she was away from her family, the dimples and smiles vanished. Her mouth drooped. Even the glowing eyes became somber and unhappy. Without the animation in her face, she looked drawn and suddenly desperately miserable.

"Thanks for not saying anything," Toni whispered. "I really appreciate it."

Merry felt a twinge of pity. Perhaps the selfish, spoiled Toni had genuinely cared for Robert, until all this unpleasantness blew up. Still, if their engagement was broken, as Sean had reported, why was she still wearing the ring? Why did the family still assume she was engaged? Merry decided to tread very carefully.

"I suppose Robert gave you the ring?" Merry remarked as she indicated Toni's hand. "It used to belong to our grandmother. They are very pretty stones, aren't they?"

Toni tipped her hand so that blue and purple sparks reflected up from the stones. "Yes," she agreed warily. "Sorry about Mother's big mouth."

"As long as my Dad and Aunt don't find out," Merry warned.

"Sean's a good sport," Toni assured her. "He'll play along."

Merry shut her mouth firmly. It was important not to antagonize Toni. She kept her opinion of Sean to herself. "Your parents seem a lot happier about your engagement?"

Toni's mouth twisted into an ugly shape. "The fact that Robert's people own a string of hotels had a lot to do with that," she said with a sneer. "He wasn't as popular as an itinerant labourer."

"Robert never went for the material things of life," Merry explained. "He said they became chains around your lifestyle!" She stood in front of the mirror beside Toni and patted a stray curl into position. She watched Toni's face. "Anyhow, I guess you've got to know Robert and his views pretty well by now?"

"Yes," Toni said flatly. She twisted her hand so that the stones sparkled again. "Is he pigheaded all the time?" she pleaded in a completely different voice.

"He has a tendency to get that way if he's pushed," Merry said carefully. What had Robert been pigheaded about with his fiancée? For a few seconds she had the curious idea that Toni was the one in the wrong, not Robert.

She remembered the fights Robert had had with his parents over the years; over wearing raggy jeans to social gatherings, over dropping out of university, and the biggest one, over working casual jobs long enough to blow accumulated money on rest and recreation. She sneaked another look at Toni's woebegone face. Toni must have been very upset to find out about Robert's dishonesty. Yet why was she still wearing the engagement ring? Why let her parents believe that she was still engaged?

"Where is he?" Merry demanded abruptly.

"He had to go away for a few days," Toni said with a shrug. She examined Merry suspiciously. "Why the third degree?"

"I thought he might have been here with you," Merry retorted.

"Well, he isn't!" Toni snapped back.

She pushed past Merry to leave the room. Merry followed more slowly. She watched as Toni's face dimpled up into its brilliant smile as though she hadn't a care in the world!

Merry studied the assured, controlled face of the vivacious dark-haired girl Robert had become involved with. She was teasing her future parents-in-law in the most unexceptional manner, so they were laughing and looked anything but the sour-faced couple Robert had called them.

Toni was hiding something, but what was it? Merry sighed, almost unaware that she had done so. If only she could find Robert and talk to him. Again she thought miserably that it was just too hard to believe that he had really stolen that forty-five thousand dollars from the company.

"A penny for them?" her uncle asked as he looked over at her.

"A two dollar coin and a cent at least," Merry retorted, rousing herself from her reverie. She had come to visit Robert's parents on an information gathering exercise. Well, so far, she had discovered that his fiancée didn't know anything about his whereabouts. Her aunt would be the next person to concentrate on, she decided. She smiled across at her aunt. "Is the weather going to clear up long enough for us to have a small game of golf?"

"We will rug up and go tomorrow anyway," her aunt promised happily, her face lighting up at the thought of her golf.

After the Gambertons left, Merry hoped they would settle quietly for the evening. The house seemed restful and pleasant, and outside the rain was still coming down, but she had forgotten about her relative's fondness for socializing. Despite Merry's protests, they insisted she come with them to a formal dinner at one of their friend's homes. So Merry had no chance to talk with her aunt alone that night.

The next morning, the rain still poured down. The game of golf was cancelled. Her uncle left after breakfast and her aunt decided that Merry should come shopping.

"You do need some new clothes," she insisted. "You won't deny me the pleasure of picking out something really special for you."

"Really, Aunt Marilyn!" Merry had protested. "All I do is work in the shop and go to bed early. I don't need any new clothes."

"Nonsense!" was the reply. "Sean will expect you to dress more appropriately once you get married."

Merry was silenced. She was very fond of her aunt, but she didn't want to have to make any complicated explanations. She blushed as she remembered the way she had responded to his kiss. Her aunt wouldn't understand anyway. It was a matter she couldn't even discuss with Aunt Adelaide and she loved and trusted her. Or perhaps, being a maiden aunt, she couldn't discuss it anyway. For not the first time she wished desperately that her mother was still alive. She needed a mother to help her work out the way she felt. She became aware that her aunt was still talking.

"I mean, dear, Tom and your Aunt Adelaide are not very worldly people. You should take your public image more seriously. Once you're married, Sean will expect..."

"I would love you to take me shopping, Aunt Marilyn," Merry interrupted. She had suddenly remembered that it was going to be an hour's drive to the big shopping centre. She was going to have time to get her aunt talking about something more important than clothes. "You don't have to convince me. Let's go!"

It took nearly the first half-hour of their journey before Merry could guide her aunt away from the engrossing subject of cocktail clothes, dinner dresses, trousseau underwear, and then the inexhaustible subject of wedding dresses.

"You are going to let us give you a wedding dress, just as a wedding present?" begged her aunt.

"No rush," Merry said. "And you are getting a very nice daughter-in-law anyway."

"Yes, she is a lovely girl," her aunt agreed. "And so suitable. Your uncle is so pleased that Robert has done the right thing."

Merry was relieved that she hadn't had to bring up the subject of Robert herself. It was now a natural progression to continue the conversation about Robert.

"Where is Robert at the moment?"

"You know Robert," her aunt replied vaguely. "He's just gone off again!"

There was a silence. The windscreen wipers fanned backwards and forwards, sweeping the water off the windscreen with a decorous hushing noise. The visibility was reduced to greyness and rain, and the headlights shone weakly on the wet road in front of them. They were enclosed in a private world. The car purred smoothly down the steep winding hill that led to the small township. It was a moment in time that seemed right for shared confidences.

"Toni seemed to think that Robert was being pigheaded about something," Merry ventured.

"You know Robert," her aunt said. She leaned forward as she drove, watching the road. A tear welled out of her eye and started its journey down her cheek. "He is pigheaded."

The car reached the bottom of the hill and turned into the side street, to plunge into the waiting cave of the underground car park. The wet weather must have discouraged other shoppers, because mostly empty parking spaces stretched their expanse into the gloom.

"What has he done this time?" Merry asked gently.

Her aunt dabbed at her face and produced her compact to repair the ravages of the one telltale tear.

"He is so pigheaded," she repeated in exasperation. "You know how he carries on?"

"He and his father have had another fight," Merry interpreted.

"This time it was not his father's fault," her aunt admitted with a sigh. "Sometimes I wonder about Robert, and engaged to this nice girl, too.'"

"What was it over this time?" Merry asked. "Is there something that any of us could do to help?"

"He turned up last Thursday night," her aunt explained. "He was driving a delivery van." Merry waited, patting her aunt on the shoulder. Her aunt took a deep breath and blew her nose. "He wanted his father to give him forty-five thousand dollars immediately."

Merry's heart sank. Despite the warmth of the car, she felt cold all over. Robert had taken the money after all and wanted to replace it before the books were audited! Her lips were almost too stiff to form her next sentence.

"I suppose Uncle Bill was upset by him demanding so much money?"

"Of course not!" was the surprising reply. "Do you think that your uncle is a pauper or something?"

Merry tried to keep her whirling confused thoughts under control. Her uncle wasn't upset about being asked for the money, so what was the problem? She remembered the key word that had triggered her aunt off.

"I know Robert is pigheaded, but what about my uncle?"

"He was welcome to twice that amount," her aunt wailed. "Robert is our only son! He is going to have everything we have one day anyway." Merry patted her aunt's shoulder and waited. Her aunt took a deep breath, dabbed at her eyes and continued trying to explain. "As Bill said, if it was to put towards a business, a home, a honeymoon, or to buy Toni a decent ring he could name his own figure."

"And?" Merry prompted.

"He refused to say what he wanted it for, so his father refused to give it to him." The tears came faster. She dabbed at her eyes ineffectually. Merry put her arms around her in sympathy. "He's so pigheaded, Merry, and don't tell a soul--not even Toni knows." She paused, and then burst out. "He's gone off working!"

"Nothing wrong with that," Merry consoled, puzzling at her aunt's genuine grief. "Lots of people work for what they want." The ever-pressing weight on her mind was gone. Relief was making her feel lightheaded. Robert wasn't going to tell his father he needed the money to make restitution and being pigheaded, had gone off to earn it. "As you say, he is pigheaded."

"You're a dear girl, Merry, but I don't think you understand," her aunt quavered. She straightened up and delved for her mirror to again repair the ravages of her tears. Her voice was steadier as she spoke again. "He has taken a job on the Bass Strait oil rigs!"

"Very adventurous, and very like Robert," Merry agreed.

"With danger money and overtime, he will have his forty-five thousand in three months," her aunt said miserably.

Suddenly, Merry understood. Robert had got himself one of the most dangerous and unpleasant jobs on the oilrig, working as an underwater welder! She remembered he had once told her that the job of underwater welder was one he would never do again!

"Dirty, unpleasant and dangerous," he had said. "There are much more entertaining things to do in life than try that again."

"Wouldn't it have been easier to give him the money?" Merry asked through stiff lips. "What if he doesn't survive long enough to inherit any of your wealth?"

"All he had to do was tell his father what he wanted it for," her aunt said with a sigh. "After all, his father has his pride, too! Robert is always expecting people to take him on trust."

"Yes," Merry agreed dryly.

She couldn't see Robert admitting what he wanted the money for, nor telling a fib to get it. Her uncle wasn't the only one who had his pride! She only hoped that her pigheaded cousin Robert wouldn't get himself killed earning the money, so that her pigheaded uncle would still have an heir to leave his money to! He could have at least explained what he was doing to Toni. She obviously was genuinely bewildered and miserable about his disappearance. Yet, the warmth and relief still flooded through her. It was nice to think that her cousin Robert was going to return the money.

"Let's do our shopping," Merry suggested at last. She smiled her reassurance at her aunt. "I'm sure he will be all right. You know Robert!"

Her aunt managed to smile back. "Of course, you're right, dear. I've been letting myself get upset quite unnecessarily. Let's cheer up and go shopping!"

Chapter 10

Merry kept a pleasant smile on her face but decided that her legs ached. She had worn shoes with heels to accompany her aunt, but it would have been more practical to have worn comfortable sneakers. She had forgotten about her aunt's zest for shopping. She had followed her in and out of innumerable boutiques, and up and down the three levels of the shopping centre, but so far their shopping excursion had been fruitless.

The rain and the lowered grey clouds gave an illusion of twilight to the day. Cars crept down the main street, headlights dimmed and yellow through the rain. All the lanes and arcades of the big shopping centre blazed with lights, remorselessly cheerful in contrast, and of course deceptive when choosing colours.

"I know it is a lovely vibrant shade, Aunt Marilyn," Merry recited over and again. "But much too bright in daylight."

Her aunt was never convinced. Merry took the vivid turquoise garment or whatever else her aunt had picked, outside to the daylight.

Her aunt shuddered and returned it to the sales assistant. "You're right, dearest, most unsuitable."

"I think we should stop and have something to eat," Merry suggested at last.

She wondered how her frail looking aunt had the energy to keep shopping with such enthusiasm hour after hour. Even on her longest day at work, when she started before dawn and finished well after seven at night, her legs, feet and head hadn't ached as much as they did after these few hours of what her aunt considered an enjoyable shopping excursion.

"We'll go to the hotel for a counter lunch," her aunt agreed. "And perhaps have a peep at the bridal shop as we go past."

Merry sighed. She had spent the entire morning steering her romantic aunt away from boutiques and bridal shops displaying wedding dresses and flimsy and impractical trousseaux. She had agreed that perhaps she needed another dinner dress, but she wasn't really contemplating marrying for quite a while, so there was plenty of time to think about wedding dresses.

"It doesn't hurt to look," her aunt had protested, her mouth drooping into a sullen pout. "I'm not going to be done out of the pleasure of helping you choose your wedding dress and trousseau."

Merry soothed her aunt with a glibness that surprised her and resolutely diverted their excursion into the search for a suitable dinner dress and matching accessories. It was just unfortunate that the small exclusive bridal emporium was between them and their counter lunch.

Merry paused under the shelter of the shop veranda. Her aunt had stopped to study the window. The brightly lit display glared out into the gloom of the grey day. The two mannequins in the window were coolly elegant and sophisticated in gleaming satins and heavy lace.

Despite herself Merry admired the display. They would suit Toni's style more than herself of course. She could just see Toni dressed in the rich sophistication and elegance of heavy satin and lace. She puzzled about Toni again.

"Merry!" her aunt called from inside the shop. "Come here! I want you to see this."

Merry sighed. One second of absentmindedness and her aunt had escaped into the shop! She walked down to the end of the shop, past the long line of bridal dresses displayed on the raised platforms. Her aunt stood by the back wall of the shop, her face radiant with triumph.

"There!" she said happily, as she gestured at the end display.

Merry smiled at her enthusiasm. Her smile wavered and grew wistful as she saw the dress. She wasn't going to marry and certainly not Sean Westwood, but if she did ever get married, she had just seen her dream wedding dress.

It was a floating white organdy, severely simple and young looking. It had a tight bodice, scooped neckline with tiny, dyed organdy flowers around it in delicate pastel colours. The billowing sleeves came in primly to fitted wrists, and the full skirt floated its width on the stand. Hand-painted flowers that matched the neckline flowers sprayed across the front of the skirt to follow the hemline around.

"Isn't it just you, Merry?" her aunt gloated. "I have never seen anything so suitable for you in my life!"

"It does look as if it would be very suitable for madam," the hovering sales assistant agreed. "Although it is only a bridesmaid's dress."

"With the right veiling and headpiece, it would be a perfect wedding dress for Merry," Aunt Marilyn decided.

Merry watched the assistant lift the wreath of matching dyed organdy flowers from the head of the mannequin, throw a veil over it and replace the wreath. She sighed at the finish the veil made to the outfit. It was perfect! One day, if she ever got married, she promised herself dreamily, that was the sort of dress she would love to wear.

"We'll take it!" her aunt said, producing her wallet of credit cards.

Merry came down to earth with a thud. The whole situation was suddenly out of control! If she ever got married, she was quite prepared to accept the present of a wedding dress from her aunt and uncle, but that time wasn't yet! She felt the hot blood flood to her face as she tried to remonstrate.

"Not so fast, Aunt Marilyn," she protested. "I mightn't be marrying for ages yet and although it is a lovely dress, it is too soon to make a decision."

"You wouldn't find anything that will suit you so well,' her aunt argued back, clutching her card, "It is so charmingly old fashioned with those long sleeves, but somehow it suits you so perfectly."

"Even if you don't get married this season, this is not a gown that will date," the sales assistant ventured. "This is a romantic and ageless style, and although it's not a wedding dress, it could have been designed just for you."

The argument went on and on. Nothing Merry could say could dissuade her aunt from buying the dress and veil.

"I can just see you in it, Merry," her aunt said happily, as she gave Merry the two distinctive boxes to hold. "You will be able to make up a delicate tracery of spring flowers for your bouquet."

"As it has been designed as a bridesmaid's dress, I will have no problems about reselling it, if you really do change your mind," the assistant assured Merry. "Personally, I'm sure you will make a refreshingly different bride in this lovely outfit."

"A good morning's work," her aunt said happily as they left the shop. "I'm so glad we came shopping today, despite that dreadful rain."

The hotel lounge was crowded with other shoppers. Merry sat down thankfully, dropping the boxes at her sore feet. Her aunt reached over to study the menu and then paused and looked across the room.

"There's Sean Westwood!" she exclaimed. She raised her voice. "Sean! Over here!"

"Remember the engagement is a secret," Merry whispered hastily to her aunt. She felt physically sick. What if her aunt babbled on about their shopping? What was Sean going to think?

Sean, casual in dark jumper and slacks sauntered over. Merry tried to get her ridiculous panic under control. At least she felt more confident facing him in her well-cut suit.

"Hello, Mrs. Townsend, Merry," he said. He gazed down at the large white boxes with 'bridal boutique' printed on them. "Been shopping?"

Merry whispered a quiet acknowledgment. Her aunt glanced down at the boxes and smiled her triumphant smile. "It has been very successful," she said. "I have just found the most beautiful outfit for Merry, but you won't be interested in that."

Sean's face darkened and his smile vanished. He just stared at Merry's aunt. "For Merry's wedding?" he echoed. One eyebrow went up in polite interest.

"Oh, dear!" Merry's aunt said in dismay. "It is supposed to be a secret isn't it, Merry?"

Sean nodded to them curtly, and turned and left the lounge in long swift strides. His face was tight with fury! Surely, he wasn't upset over the trivial matter of her aunt's shopping? Not that it was really any of his business if her aunt chose to buy her the wedding dress of her dreams.

"He rushed off in a hurry, didn't he?' Merry's aunt said puzzled. "He seemed almost rude!"

"I think he's busy with the auditing," Merry said as she reached for the shelter of the menu. She hid behind it until the high colour on her face had died down.

"Probably busy with his house," her aunt chattered on. "I believe he had it completely renovated and refurnished in the last few months. You'll love it, Merry. He's redone it in the original Edwardian style. It's a wonder he hasn't taken you to see it yet."

"Perhaps he wanted it to be a surprise," Merry suggested faintly.

She had something to ponder over as they ordered and ate their lunch. How had he explained the forged cheques to the auditors, even if he had replaced the money? She was surprised and uneasy at the way he had rushed off without finishing the conversation.

After lunch the rain eased and they seemed to find boutiques with a more suitable selection of dresses for Merry to choose from. Merry managed to limit her aunt to one soft lilac wool dress, a selection of scarves and belts for accessories, and one severely simple golden silk evening dress. They were making their way back to the car park with all the parcels when they were stopped.

"Carry your parcels, lady?" suggested a hoarse voice.

"Jerry!" her aunt exclaimed. "Do you remember Jerry, Merry?"

Merry stared. She was convinced that she had never seen the heavily built, swarthy young man in her life. His brown eyes twinkled at the expression on her face, and somehow, another face built itself around the recognizable twinkle; a narrow, olive-skinned face with well-defined high, arched brows and a mass of black curls. The years fell away.

"Jerry Willis," she identified.

"Didn't recognize the young lady with Mrs. Townsend," he said with a laugh. "Grown up at last, Merry!"

"And you've grown out," she declared. She held out her hand to the childhood companion of Robert. "What have you been doing to grow so large?"

"Keeping out of mischief," he drawled.

"Jerry became a professional diver years ago," her aunt explained. "He was the one who helped Robert get his certificates for diving."

"Robert around these days?" was the next question, as their parcels were stacked neatly into the boot of the car.

"He wants his whereabouts kept secret," Merry's aunt warned. "He is doing a three-month stint underwater welding in Bass Strait."

"Not like the old Robert to soil his hands at welding," was the comment. "Not like the old Robert at all," he repeated. "Tell him to drop in to see me when he's off shift." He tugged at his ear, a characteristic Merry remembered denoted worry. "I'm home until the end of the month."

"Won't he be there for the three months?" Merry demanded.

"He will get enough time off between shifts to get home for a few hours," Jerry said. He grinned, showing startling white teeth. "Last time I saw him, he was staying out of mischief with a fiery little brunette."

"Toni Gamberton, and they are engaged," Merry's aunt said proudly. "Drop in if you're passing," she suggested. "It's been a long time."

Merry waved back to him as they left. "Haven't seen Jerry since he was twelve," she remembered.

"He and Robert were inseparable," her aunt agreed. "Hasn't he grown into a big boy? Suppose it is all that swimming. Are you going to wear your new dress to the Golf Club evening tonight?"

"We're going out?" Merry asked in humorous dismay. "I found today very exhausting. Aren't you just a little bit tired?"

"Shopping revitalizes me," her aunt confided. "I always do it when I'm bored or not feeling well. I'm just so happy about securing that dress for your wedding." She sneaked a quick glance at Merry's pensive face. "Look! I didn't mean to ram it down your throat, but it is so very you. I just couldn't resist it. I'll not say a word about it again, until you decide on a wedding date."

"If you promise you won't say a word," Merry warned, deciding she was going to have to accept her impulsive aunt's purchase.

Her aunt would be disappointed when eventually she found out that there wasn't going to be a wedding. Perhaps one day, she would meet someone she wanted to marry, and that beautiful, romantic, dreamy just-right dress could be waiting for her. For some reason, a sharp pang twisted at her heart, but it was gone before she could analyze what had caused it.

"Promise," her aunt with a smile, "A secret between us, then."

The Golf Club and the Country Club seemed to be the centre of the social life around the district, Merry decided in resignation. There was the dinner that night and on Saturday the Country Club dinner and dance. Her aunt and uncle protested loudly when she talked of going home on Saturday.

"Old Tom and Adelaide can spare you another few hours," her uncle grumbled. "You haven't been down here for months. Don't rush off."

"I want to go home for a rest," Merry explained. "All this sleeping in and socializing is very exhausting."

However, that night Merry was more resigned to going out when she tried on her new gold silk dress. Staying with her aunt and uncle always made her feel like Cinderella. The dress really was very becoming; almost Grecian with the one bare shoulder and the draped look to it. She curled her hair up into a chignon, and admired the borrowed, exactly matching amber earrings. She looked very sophisticated.

"Very nice," her uncle approved. "You are growing up into a very attractive young lady, Merry." He then spoiled his compliment by continuing. "I don't know why you insist on grubbing around in the business. Tom could employ someone."

"I happen to like--no love, working in the business, Uncle Bill," Merry almost snorted. "It is what I trained to do and Dad couldn't budge me even if he tried."

"Just passing a remark," her uncle said meekly. "Let's go."

The Country Club was crowded. Merry started to recognize the faces. There were acquaintances and friends of her aunt and uncle, and the occasional school friend of Robert. Everyone exclaimed over how Merry had grown up and some of Robert's friends came over to dance with her. Jerry arrived and danced with her, bulking large in his dinner jacket.

"So Robert wanted money that badly?" Jerry muttered in his hoarse voice as soon as they were on the floor.

"Keep it quiet, Jerry," Merry warned. "Not even Toni knows about it."

"I don't like it," Jerry grumbled. Merry looked a question. Jerry shrugged. "You know Robert," he finished lamely.

Merry sighed at that. Why did everyone have to come out with that particular phrase and in that particular tone about her cousin all the time? Jerry had always been his best friend. She stared into his worried dark eyes. Worried! Why was he worried about Robert? He would have taught Robert everything he knew about diving!

"What's wrong with Robert doing that particular job?" she demanded.

Jerry avoided her eyes and started to steer her back to her table. "He did get his certificate," he admitted. "Not much experience. His luck is going to run out one of these days."

Merry stopped abruptly. The laughing crowd swirled around them, as the band started another number. Remembering Robert and his attitude towards not taking anything seriously, she had suddenly interpreted Jerry's words.

"He's not properly qualified for that job, is he?" she demanded.

"It's not a job for amateurs," Jerry said evasively as he returned her to the table, and fled any further questions.

The evening went on and on. More and more people arrived. Between dances and conversation, Merry pondered over what Jerry had admitted. Underwater welding wasn't a job for amateurs--and Robert was the most dedicated amateur she had ever known. Yet there was nothing she could do except wait. She yawned behind her hand. She decided that she was tired, and wondered how soon it would be before they would be able to go home.

She looked across the room and noticed without any particular interest that Toni and her mother and father had arrived to join a crowded table. Toni was eye-catching in a clinging, silver lame dress, and apparently in very high spirits. She immediately moved onto the dance floor with Jerry Willis.

"What are the Gambertons doing at your Country Club?" Merry asked her uncle, who was sitting beside her.

"This is the country, Merry," he explained. "Everybody knows everybody else! Isn't that Sean with them? I thought you said he wasn't coming down for the weekend?"

Merry stared across the room, shocked out of her tiredness. Sean Westwood, elegant in a black dinner jacket, was coming over!

"Remember that the engagement is supposed to be a secret and don't say anything," she whispered urgently to her uncle.

Sean greeted all the people he seemed to know sitting at their table and held out his hand in an invitation for Merry to dance. She moistened her lips to refuse him, but he had already pulled her to her feet, and was guiding her smoothly across the room, with the precision and lightness that she remembered.

"I wanted to have a few words with you," he said quietly.

He smiled at Toni, flirting blatantly with Jerry, and nodded to other couples, but all the time he guided her around the floor to the other side of the room, down a curtained off passage and through into a deserted room. The latch clicked loudly as he shut the door behind him.

"I'm sure you will be relieved to know that the delivery van turned up," he said. "Abandoned at the small airfield."

"So he didn't steal it, just borrowed it," Merry retorted.

Her cold panic evaporated. She felt a sense of relief that the van had turned up. With Robert you were never quite sure all the time. He didn't have the usual respect towards other people's property.

"Yes, but where is he?" Sean asked thoughtfully. "He has an interesting choice of places to get to from that field."

"He will replace the company money, I swear," Merry said. *So Robert had caught a helicopter across to his job at the Bass Strait rig*, she pondered. She looked again at Sean. "Just trust him."

"Trust him!" Sean echoed. Suddenly his temper seemed to get the better of his tight self-control. He started pacing up and down as he burst out. "Do I look like a fool? I don't trust him or you either! I don't want any scandal, but he won't get away with such blatant thieving, not if I follow him to the ends of the earth."

"You won't need to go to the ends of the earth," Merry flung back, enraged beyond caution and then put her hand over her mouth in horror. She had nearly betrayed Robert with her stupid retort.

Sean stopped pacing to swing around, "So you do know where he is, don't you?" he accused.

"He's going to replace the money," Merry flung back. "Why are you so intent on hounding him?"

"Because he's a liar, a thief, and a user." Sean's voice was low and even. "He has used old Tom, Adelaide, his parents and Toni. Why have you so little self-respect that you let him use you as well?"

"You will get your money back." Merry thought of Robert working in a dangerous and unpleasant job for which he wasn't sufficiently qualified, just to return the money and her rage nearly choked her. "I can't bear to keep seeing you hurt so much in your hip pocket! You really have your priorities straight, haven't you? Rushing around accusing all and sundry of thieving from you?"

"Little Miss Innocence," he said. "Where is Robert Townsend? What are you both up to with my forty-five thousand dollars?" His voice slowed to a bitter mocking drawl. "Apart from buying wedding finery of course!"

"Stuff your forty-five thousand dollars," Merry shrieked back at him, too infuriated to realize how her voice had risen. She slapped his face with all her strength. He clenched his fists and stared at her.

"You're mean spirited, suspicious and filthy minded," Merry raged. "Wallow like the pig you are in your nasty suspicions. I don't have to talk to you--ever again."

She ran past him, tugged the door open and fled the room. She wanted desperately to weep, as if somehow she had accidentally broken something precious--which under the circumstances was ridiculous!

Chapter 11

Merry sped along the quiet passage and pushed through crowds of laughing people, heading to the other side of the room to the shelter of the ladies room. To her relief it was deserted.

It was only then she felt the tremor go through her body. Then she started to shake properly. She sat in front of a mirror and stared blankly at her reflection. Muffled by the shut door, the soft dance music became an accompaniment to her thudding pulse.

The sleek, assured sophisticated image was gone. It was a much younger, more vulnerable, Merry Land who stared back, biting her lower lip. She was white-faced, her eyes glittering with the threat of unshed tears. Her hair tumbled down around her shoulders and cascaded down her back.

She tried taking deep breaths to steady herself. The nausea from the cold pit of her stomach spread. She clenched her teeth. She was not going to let herself be made physically sick by the fight with Sean Westwood! She clung to the cold edge of the hand basin. Slowly the nausea and trembling subsided.

She splashed cold water across her face and waited. Soon, her breathing steadied, and the tremors lessened. She inspected herself. A frown wrinkled her brow. She was a mess! She didn't have her purse and make-up with her to hide the damage. She couldn't even comb her hair before she left the protection of the ladies room.

She was carefully blotting her face dry with a tissue when Toni entered. Her dimples and flashing smile were gone, and her face looked drawn and almost haggard. She looked startled when she realized Merry was watching her.

"Hello," she said lamely.

She sat down beside Merry, applied silver glitter above her eyes and used her lipstick. She ran a small brush through her hair. Suddenly her eyes strayed to Merry's rigid reflection beside her.

"You were with Sean," she said. She turned. Her sharp eyes inspected Merry more closely. "Have you had a fight with him?"

"Is it that obvious?" Merry asked.

"Really, darling!" Toni drawled.

"He seemed to think I knew where Robert is," Merry explained.

"And do you?" Toni whispered.

Merry looked into the desperate entreaty of Toni's eyes. Robert's disappearance must have upset Toni, despite the fact that it was she who had broken the engagement. Then she remembered that the reason Sean was after Robert was because of Toni's accusation and hardened her heart.

"He's chasing Robert for the forty-five thousand dollars he embezzled," she said evading the question.

"Tilt your face further back," Toni said as she applied eye makeup, and then blusher to Merry's face. She stepped back and studied her. "The lights are pretty dim outside, so I think you will get by." In a sudden change of tone, she said bitterly. "Sean won't let go once he's on the trail. He will follow until the bitter end!"

"Sean said you broke off your engagement?" Merry probed her eyes on the familiar ring on Toni's hand.

"Sean's not that bad, you know," Toni said, her head averted as she carefully packed away her makeup. "Usually he's a pretty solid citizen." She sneaked an anxious sidelong glance at Merry. "It's just that when he gets an idea in his head, he hangs on to it."

"And Robert never gets involved in arguments," Merry wondered aloud. "He says they take too much energy."

Toni looked at her sharply. She took a deep breath, and her next sentence came out as a fast garbled rush. "If you see him, tell him I didn't mean what I did and that I love him."

"I don't expect to see him," Merry said.

Toni wasn't listening. As they walked out and into the big room, the dance music and crowded room had transformed her back into a radiant and vivacious girl, already flirting with the two young men who had pounced on her as she appeared.

Merry moved back to her table thoughtfully. Toni seemed a very complex person. She was shallow, spoilt and self-centred. She had denounced Robert and broken her engagement, but still wore his ring. She claimed that she loved him and she had just been unexpectedly supportive to Merry.

Merry's aunt was yawning, and she greeted Merry's arrival with relief. "Merry, my love, can we drag you away or do you want to stay for a while longer?"

"It's been a lovely evening, but I am tired," Merry returned. "I want to get an early start tomorrow to go home."

"It was a lovely evening," her aunt agreed dreamily as they were driven home by the yawning Bill Townsend. "You look really lovely in that gold dress, Merry. You should wear that colour more often. What happened to

Sean? I saw him leave after his dance with you. I had thought that he would be more attentive?"

"You're a born romantic," Merry teased with a lightness that she wasn't feeling. Who else had noticed her flight into the ladies room, or Sean's abrupt departure? "Remember I see him every day through work." *But not if I can help it,* Merry promised herself silently.

Sean Westwood was nothing but a vindictive and detestable man and she would make sure that he never upset her again. A shiver went through her as she remembered Toni's reluctant admission that when he got an idea into his head he hung onto it. What would happen if Robert was unable to earn the full amount he had to return? Would Sean really hound him remorselessly forever?

"You're shivering," her aunt discovered. She turned the car heater up. "Never mind," she comforted. "We'll soon be home, and get you tucked up snugly." She returned to her original complaint. "Do you really have to go back tomorrow? I'm sure Tom and Adelaide can spare you for another few days. Also, that rain isn't going to ease up and I don't like you driving home in it."

Merry hugged her aunt. "I've loved being down here," she assured her. "But I want to get back home. It is time for Cinderella to turn back into a pumpkin."

"Wish you'd let me get you a decent car," her uncle grumbled, overhearing their conversation. "I hate you driving that heap."

"It's road-worthy," Merry said with a laugh. "Waste not, want not, Uncle Bill. How am I ever going to grow as rich as you if I'm not thrifty when young?"

This was greeted with the amusement she had hoped, and once again he was diverted from his grievance about her battered Mini.

In the morning, after an affectionate farewell from her aunt and uncle, when she was half an hour into her journey home, but still driving past the isolated paddocks outside the metropolitan area, she had occasion to regret her words. The windscreen wipers of the Mini faltered and then stopped under the heavy load of the continuous water pouring over the windscreen.

She pulled over to the side of the road in exasperation. Without windscreen wipers, the visibility was too limited for safe driving. Around her was nothing but paddocks stretching away into the greyness of the heavy rain. No houses, no shops, no phones and no passing traffic. She took out her mobile and looked at it in dismay. She had forgotten to recharge it!

She studied the threatening darkness of the low clouds and sighed. She was going to have to wait out the weather. Her nice early start was wasted! It might be hours before the rain cleared enough for her to drive.

She turned off the engine. The car got colder. She dragged the old blanket from the back seat and huddled into it. An hour went past, and then another. The rain showed no sign of easing. She looked at her watch. She just had to get home! If she didn't arrive as expected her father and Aunt Adelaide would start to worry. She decided to give the rain another half-hour, and then trudge to the nearest phone.

However, she only got a short distance up the road, huddled in the shelter of her duffel coat and hood when the grey bulk of a Mercedes purred up beside her. Merry saw the familiar figure behind the wheel and her heart sank. Of all people to be using the road, she fumed. She stared straight ahead and kept walking. The car purred slowly along beside her. The offside window wound down.

"What's wrong?" Sean's voice asked.

"My windscreen wipers packed up," she said shortly.

"I'll drive you home."

"I can manage, thank you," she said, still without looking at him as she trudged along.

"You don't look as if you are managing," was his good humoured reply.

"What I do is no business of yours," Merry snapped.

"Your father rang Bill Townsend to say you hadn't arrived home. He and your aunt were frantic. Bill Townsend phoned to ask me to keep an eye open for you," Sean explained. "A bit unnecessary to worry them any more isn't it?"

Merry bit her lips. She had overlooked the obvious fact that her Aunt Marilyn would have rung immediately she had left to say she was on her way. She had forgotten about how over-protective everyone was! She glanced at her watch. They would have expected her to arrive about an hour ago. They must have rung through to her aunt and uncle almost as soon as she didn't turn up when expected. Predictably Bill Townsend would have rung Sean to look out for her. She was being childish again.

The Mercedes stopped. Merry opened the door and got into the car. When she shut the door the window wound up silently. The car purred to a stop outside the garage in the small township. Two men sitting in the office over their steaming mugs of coffee stared at the Mercedes but didn't move. As the Mercedes had stopped away from the pumps it was obvious that it didn't need petrol and the men weren't going to brave the rain for whatever else was wanted.

"Give me your car keys, and wait here," Sean ordered.

He got out of the car and sprinted for the shelter of the office. Merry watched the short conversation and nods of agreement. He scribbled a note and handed it to them. Even before he had returned to the car, the tow truck was leaving the shelter of the garage to drive back down the highway towards her stranded Mini.

"I should really wait for them to bring it back and fix it," Merry decided. "I'm going to need it tomorrow."

"I have an employee who lives in the township. He will drive it to the city tomorrow and drop it at your shop," Sean explained. "So there is no need for you to hang around to wait for its repair."

"There is the matter of paying for the repairs and tow truck," Merry pointed out, unreasonably irked by his competence. "I don't really wish to lean on your hip pocket nerve."

His cheeks tinged a darker red. She realized that she had scored a hit under his armour of good humour.

"Your RACV will cover the towing and as the Mini is a company registered vehicle, the repairs will be covered under the normal Westwood and Merriland's garage expenses." He glanced at her. "So my hip pocket nerve is quite protected."

Merry was silenced. The car purred along smoothly, and the silence lengthened. She wished she hadn't been provoked into making that comment about his hip pocket nerve. It had made her sound childish and put her at a disadvantage. After the dreadful fight they had had the previous evening, she felt nervous and unsure in his presence.

This man had the power to provoke a depth of unsuspected emotion in her. Never before had her temper or rage managed to over-ride her self-control so completely. It was an unknown, undisciplined facet of her personality that frightened her with its intensity. Unbidden, the memory of their night at the cottage, his warm lips, and the abandoned way she had clung to him and returned his kiss crept into her mind. She flushed at the memory, despite herself, and huddled further down in the seat, staring fixedly at the hypnotic sweep of the windscreen wipers.

After a while, she became aware that they had stopped and the engine was turned off. She had been so immersed in her own thoughts that she hadn't noticed the time or distance passed. Were they home already? She released her seatbelt almost automatically.

"I said," he repeated, and she became aware that she hadn't been listening to his previous words. She looked at him questioningly. He sounded awkward, almost stilted as he spoke. "That I wanted to apologize for losing my temper last night. Your indignation and reaction was quite justified."

"Yes," Merry muttered.

She studied the windscreen. The drops of water splattered and then filled the fan shaped clear patch in front of her. She wondered should she apologize for the hard slap she had delivered, but the words wouldn't force themselves past her stiff lips.

"Merry!" he said. His hand reached for her chin and turned her face towards him. "Look at me, Merry! I am so sorry about last night. Robert's whereabouts aren't that important to me."

Merry stared into the gold-flecked grey eyes. They were surrounded with thick black lashes. Much too thick and attractive to be wasted on a man. A heritage of some Irish forebears, an irrelevant part of her mind decided. Her thoughts and actions seem suspended in a dream like limbo. He reached over and pulled her towards him.

"Oh, Merry darling," he groaned. "Is Robert that important to you?"

He kissed her captured hands, and then her nose. Then his lips were on her mouth, evoking the frighteningly familiar dreamy lassitude. Everything faded to unimportance except the emotions he was evoking. Her undisciplined arms strayed up around his neck to pull him closer. It was at that point, that the offside door was swung open and the cold wind, wetness and her father's voice flooded in to break the spell that held her captive.

"We have been so worried," her father started to say before his voice trailed into astonished silence.

As Sean's arms dropped away from around her, Merry suddenly became aware of exactly what the scene must look like from her father's eyes. The car had stopped, but no one had got out. Her father had hurried from the house with the big umbrella and opened the door. His daughter was cuddled into their business partner's embrace, pulling him close in a passionate kiss. Merry started to blush. The heat from her blush spread. She felt her whole body blazed with her embarrassment and shame. What was her father going to think of her? Why was that passionate, exciting stranger hiding inside her able to spring into existence as soon as Sean touched her?

With a muttered excuse she slid out of the car, pushed past her father, and ran headlong through the heavy rain into the house. She ran past the startled Aunt Adelaide without a word. She didn't stop running until she reached the sanctuary of her own bedroom. Only then did the tears start.

Chapter 12

All the next week Aunt Adelaide and her father were unusually quiet. Merry noticed that they watched her all the time but had very little to say. She braced herself as she waited for the inevitable questions about the incident in Sean's car, but no one said anything.

The Mini was returned to its usual spot by the shop on Monday morning, but there was no sign of Sean that week. She supposed he was still involved with the auditors. Another young man appeared from the office to check their supplies and collect the banking.

Merry was relieved by Sean's prolonged absence, but for some obscure reason it annoyed her. The cold wet spell was over, and the sun came out brilliantly and cheerfully warm. She very quickly became too busy to even think about him. The firm of Westwood and Merriland's were back into the business of romance again. The orders came in and kept on coming; for bouquets, posies, and long-stemmed roses and Merry worked later and later each afternoon on the flower arrangements.

A nervous young apprentice called Sylvia arrived to help Merry and her aunt with the backlog of orders. She had an artistic flair for putting the arrangements together, but she was painfully shy, and worked in silence for most of the time.

"I'm glad that you had that break last week, Merry," Aunt Adelaide declared as she handed around mugs of coffee after the particularly frantic Friday morning. "We certainly wouldn't have been able to spare you this week."

"Amazing the difference a rise in the temperature makes," Merry agreed. "Have you put in the order for the extra roses?"

"Might be arriving now." Aunt Adelaide peered through the window as the familiar long, white van pulled up out the front.

The deliveryman came in with the stacked boxes and put them in the small room behind the counter. "Six dozen roses and a parcel for Miss Merry," he said, as he put it on the counter on his way out.

"Must be the new receipt books," Aunt Adelaide suggested. "They look smaller than the last lot. Open them up, Merry."

"Feels too light to be books," Merry said as she handled the box.

"Open it up," Aunt Adelaide ordered.

Merry pulled the flimsy tissue off the box. A pale pink orchid with a deeper pink throat nestled in the greenery of fern around it. It was a very intriguing little spray. She lifted it out. There was no card in the box.

"One of Tom's orchids," her aunt suggested.

Sylvia who was leaning over Merry's shoulder to admire the spray, stifled a giggle. Merry looked at her. Sylvia flushed pinkly and started unpacking the roses.

"Tom must have sent over one of the first lot that flowered," Aunt Adelaide said. "Must be one of those hybrids he was talking about!"

"Very pretty," Merry agreed, as she put the orchid in a vase on the counter. "Nice to know what Dad's been working on all these weeks."

However, that night, when her father came home, he looked surprised at her thanks, and denied sending it.

"My hybrids won't be flowering for a few weeks yet," he explained. "Must be one of Sean's lot."

Merry realized that her aunt and father were watching her with questioning looks. The silence in the shabby but cozy living room lengthened. They waited for her to say something. Merry thought of how silent and watchful they both had been all the week since her return on the Sunday.

To her horror she felt her cheeks redden. They were assuming that the gift of the pink orchid was from Sean! Would he have sent her the pink orchid, and if so, why?

"There was no note or card," Merry managed at last.

"A mystery admirer," Aunt Adelaide suggested dryly, too dryly, Merry sensed.

"Be one of Sean's new orchids," her father confirmed. "His batch have already started flowering." He yawned and looked at the time. "I'm for bed. See you in the morning."

"A good idea," Merry responded with relief. "Think I'll get an early night as well."

"A few minutes of your time, Merry," Aunt Adelaide suggested meaningfully. She waited until Tom's bedroom door closed after him before she spoke again. "Marilyn rang on Sunday to let us know what time you left there."

"Very thoughtful of her," Merry agreed. Her pulse started to speed up. She had a suspicion of what was coming. Her Aunt Marilyn couldn't keep anything secret to save her life. Her aunt's next words confirmed her worst suspicions.

"She did tell me that for some reason you were keeping your engagement to Sean Westwood a secret! Why? Is there any reason you don't want us to know about it? You must know that neither your father nor I have any objection to Sean. We think you both would be very well suited."

"It's just that..." Merry floundered, remembering the witnessed kiss last Sunday. Her father would have been sure to have told her aunt about it and of course the pink orchid, if it was from Sean, was damning! She wondered with an unaccustomed apprehension if her Aunt Marilyn had also mentioned the wedding dress hidden in the back of the built in wardrobe at Winterview?

"I'm not really sure," she confessed with perfect truth, suddenly glad to be able to bring at least some of her doubts into the open. "He can be very nice, but he is also managing, tenacious and single-minded. He makes me nervous," she finished lamely, deciding she couldn't exactly tell her aunt that these qualities worried her with regard to Robert's' uncertain future.

"I understand your reservations," Aunt Adelaide admitted. "But those qualities aren't automatically bad! Sean isn't shallow and he is very levelheaded. You would always be able to depend on him if things went wrong." She studied Merry closely, a faint worry wrinkling her brow. "Do you think perhaps you should have waited a bit longer before making a decision?"

"Yes," Merry said baldly. She grasped at the excuse with relief. "That's why I didn't want to get official until I had thought it over."

"You should have told us," her aunt said with a sigh. "Surely you can trust us, Merry?"

"You know I do," Merry assured her. "It was Toni's parents who told Aunt Marilyn. Now can we pretend that this conversation hasn't happened?"

Of course, Merry thought to herself after she had taken herself off to bed, it wasn't going to be as easy as that! From now on, her aunt and father would be watching her and their new business partner like hawks, trying to work out what was happening between them. What had possessed Sean to go along with it so smoothly? The question went around and around in her head, until she fell asleep, to dream of parading through an infinity of weddings to shadowy grooms in her secret wedding dress.

On Saturday, Merry worked long after Aunt Adelaide and Sylvia had finished. Several of the weddings had required flower arrangements in the reception rooms, so it was quite late in the afternoon before she returned home.

The new brown Volvo Sean had insisted that her father drive and her aunt's small white sedan were already parked in the driveway. So also was the distinctive sporty red Lamborghini.

Merry turned into the drive to park behind it. What was Toni doing here? Perhaps Robert had returned? With this hope she hurried into the house, but it was only Toni drinking coffee and eating hot scones in the living room. She gave an impression of animated vivacity, all sparkling eyes and dimples at her captive audience of Tom and Aunt Adelaide.

"Here she is now," she said brightly. "Hope you aren't too exhausted, Merry, but I've come up to take you back to our place for the night."

"Why?" Merry asked blankly.

"Mummy and Daddy thought it would be nice if you could come down," Toni chattered on. Her red lips stretched their extravagant dimpled smile, but her black eyes were wary. "I'm having a few friends in for the evening."

Merry opened her mouth to refuse. She remembered Toni's friends and decided that she didn't really want to renew her acquaintance with them.

Besides, she realized as she sat down slowly and took the proffered mug of coffee from Aunt Adelaide, that she was tired, very tired.

"Please don't say no," Toni begged. Her eyes were suddenly genuinely anxious, almost frantic. "It's just a few close friends for a kitchen tea, and I desperately want you to come."

"For your wedding, dear?" Aunt Adelaide asked. "I do think that you should make the effort and go, Merry. It was very nice of the Gambertons to invite you along."

Merry looked at the pleased smile on her aunt's face and the desperation in Toni's eyes as they waited for her to answer. She nodded a slow acceptance. A kitchen tea probably meant just a few close girlfriends. Toni wasn't really that bad when you got to know her better, even if she was dreadfully self-centred.

"I'll pack an overnight bag," she agreed. "When do you want to leave?"

"As soon as possible," Toni said almost desperately, and then she giggled. "I mean, I am dying for you to see what Daddy and Mummy are giving me for a wedding present, and it is a long drive."

"You'd better put on some warm clothes, if you are traipsing all over the countryside," her aunt ordered.

Merry sighed. She went into her bedroom and changed into her smart woollen slacks, lemon shirt, and her heavy duffel coat. She packed her new misty blue woollen dress and accessories and a change of underwear.

"I'll have her back by tomorrow afternoon," Toni promised. She dropped a light hand on to Merry's arm as they went out the door. As soon as they were outside Merry flinched as Toni's sharp fingers bit into her arm, almost dragging her to the Lamborghini.

Merry threw her case over the back and took her car keys from her handbag. "I'll shift the Mini," she suggested.

"Don't bother," Toni snapped as she pulled Merry into the sheepskin covered passenger seat. "I can get around it!"

Tom and Adelaide stood at the front door and waved. The red car glided forward half a length, jerked into reverse and backed over the lawn, barely missing Tom's precious bush roses, around the Mini, and into the road.

Merry just had time to wave back as Toni accelerated the car and sped off.

"Why the hurry?" Merry demanded, as the car streaked through the suburban streets at a pace that was well above the legal speed limit.

Toni slowed to a more sedate speed. She glanced at Merry. Merry was shocked at the change in her. Without the flashing eyes and the dimples, Toni looked dreadful! Her face was so haggard it was sharp featured, and under the skilfully applied make-up her skin looked a tight stretched and unhealthy grey.

"The kitchen tea isn't until next Saturday," Toni admitted. "You're the only person who can help me, Merry! I came straight up to get you!"

"Help you?" Merry echoed blankly. She looked at the spoilt, pampered, wealthy girl, who had everything she desired lavished on her and could call on whatever help she required. What could she do to help Toni Gamberton? Then she studied the drooping mouth and the lines of strain on her face. "Okay, then, what is it?"

"It's Robert!" Toni burst out. She sneaked a look at the doubt on Merry's face. "Please, Merry! You know where he is! I know you don't want Sean to know but something's happened to him and you don't realize how important it is for me to see him!"

"What do you mean something's happened to him?" Merry temporized.

She had no intention of betraying Robert's whereabouts, always remembering that it was Toni who had betrayed him to Sean. The volatile

Toni probably wanted to make up, but if Robert rejected her, she would just as quickly betray him again if she had the information.

"You don't understand!" Toni said desperately. "I know he's had an accident! All his mother can do is to weep! She won't tell anyone where he is." Her hands shook and Merry put a restraining hand on the car wheel to straighten its course. "What if he dies before he knows I'm sorry?"

An accident! Merry's heart sank. She remembered Jerry's troubled gesture when he heard about Robert's job. He knew exactly how inexperienced Robert was to do that job, and he was unhappy about it. The more she thought about it, the sicker she felt. An accident in that line of work was often fatal! Poor Aunt! Marilyn must have fallen to pieces when she heard about it.

Merry saw the car park on the side of the road. She gestured for Toni to drive in. It was still crowded. Toni swung around several lanes before finding a vacant spot. She turned the engine off.

"Please, Merry!" she begged.

Merry tried taking deep breaths to still her own panic. It wasn't going to help to fall to pieces like her aunt as well. She had to think! Surely it couldn't be fatal? Aunt Marilyn would have had to let everyone know if he had died. He must be injured, perhaps badly, but surely he wouldn't be dead!

Her Aunt Marilyn didn't know about the breach between Toni and Robert, and yet she had refused to tell his fiancée where Robert was. Of course if she had seen Robert, he might have warned her not to tell Toni his whereabouts!

"What if he doesn't want to see you?"

"After the fight we had last time, I know he doesn't want to see me," Toni admitted. "But I've got to see him to tell him that I was wrong, and I am prepared to go along with whatever he says." A sob choked her voice. "For the rest of my life, if he will only forgive me."

"What if he still doesn't want to see you?" Merry pressed on. "What if you want to know where he is to tell Sean?"

"Please, Merry, trust me!" Toni implored. Her dark eyes were brilliant with the unshed tears. "I swear I would never say anything to Sean. You've got to help me."

"You had better be telling the truth," Merry said grimly. "It's my neck on the line if Robert isn't convinced that he wants to see you."

"I am telling the truth," Toni said with an odd dignity.

"I suppose he was working under an assumed name," Merry said slowly, thinking aloud. "He often does. If several people have been hurt in the accident and been sent to different hospitals, it still wouldn't help to find out exactly where they were sent. If Aunt Marilyn has been warned not to say where he is, she probably won't even tell me anyway."

"What about his friends?" Toni begged. "Is there anyone he is close to?"

Merry started to shake her head. Robert had lots of acquaintances, but very few close friends. Then she remembered! Jerry would know his whereabouts! He had worked on that rig! He would hear all the details about the accident. He also had no reason not to tell Robert's cousin and fiancée his whereabouts--unless he had been to visit Robert and had the same instructions as her Aunt Marilyn.

"Are you all right to drive?" Merry demanded. "We're going to visit Jerry Willis."

Toni nodded. She drove the car out of the car park. Merry was nervous of her driving, but she drove steadily and competently down the freeway, and across the mountain, and guided by Merry, at last reached the small cottage overlooking the ocean beach where Jerry lived.

"You wait in the car," Merry ordered.

She went up the path and the steps to the porch and knocked on the door. It was opened by a tall grey-haired woman who held herself very erect.

"Mrs. Willis," Merry asked. "Is Jerry around?"

"It is young Merry Land, isn't it?" Mrs. Willis exclaimed with delight. "Haven't grown much taller, have you, my dear? In you come."

"I'm in a hurry," Merry apologized. "Where's Jerry?"

"Been called back to work at the rig," was the reply. "Six men were injured in the accident, so all the boys off have gone back to help do the repairs."

Merry felt the blood drain from her face. It was one thing to hear Toni allege that had been an accident, and another thing to hear it confirmed from the matter-of-fact lips of Jerry's mother, who had lived with her son's dangerous occupations since he had first started diving.

"I forgot!" Mrs. Willis said in concern. "Of course you must be dreadfully worried about poor Robert?"

"We're just going to visit him," Merry forced out through her stiff lips.

"He must be improving if he is allowed visitors," was the reply. "Is he still down at the Trafalgar Base Hospital?"

"Nice seeing you again, Mrs. Willis," Merry babbled. "We really have to go. Remember me to Jerry."

Merry didn't hear Mrs. Willis's reply. She had turned and fled to the car. Toni waited for her to speak, a look of anxious inquiry on her face. Merry remained silent until she had controlled her trembling. If Robert wasn't allowed visitors he must be really bad!

"He's at the Trafalgar Base Hospital," she said at last, as calmly as she could manage.

"How badly is he hurt?" Toni asked as she started up the car.

"Mrs. Willis didn't know," Merry replied with perfect truth.

Merry was busy with her own thoughts for the entire two-hour drive across to the hospital. She was remembering all the gruesome stories Robert had told her about diving accidents, about the bends, and underwater explosions and falling girders. She sneaked a sidelong look at Toni. What if Robert was badly crippled, or hideously burned or blinded? Would Toni's love last the shock of seeing him?

By the time they had reached the hospital, it was dark. Merry pulled her duffel coat on over her jumper as she swung out of the car. Toni seemed unaware of the cold, and Merry had to run to keep up with her as they hurried towards the reception desk.

There was no Robert Townsend among the accident victims from the rig and the young receptionist was becoming impatient with the list of names Merry thought up. Toni drooped, looking more and more miserable as the receptionist denied knowing any of the names. At last Merry remembered about Robert's silly sense of humor. How would he swap his name around for the ocean job?

"What about Bert Tewne?"

There was a Bert Tewne! Toni's face lit up and then darkened as the receptionist looked up his case history. No visitors allowed except for immediate family. Toni volunteered the information that she was his fiancée in a faint voice. The receptionist just shrugged as she explained that Mr. Tewne had to be kept very quiet until the specialist had seen him again.

"What injuries did he sustain?" Merry asked woodenly.

The receptionist hesitated, and then said ungraciously that Mr. Tewne was out of danger. His shattered leg had been set as well as possible and his broken ribs were not causing him that much discomfort. She paused, but the anguish in Toni's eyes dragged out of her the fact that the specialist who had operated that afternoon, was not prepared to make any promises about his sight, not yet.

Toni let out an anguished groan. Merry held her tightly. So that was why poor Aunt Marilyn was in such a state of collapse! There was the danger that Robert might end up blind! How could the independent Robert manage without eyesight? The receptionist admitted they could talk to the specialist after he had seen Robert in the morning. Perhaps there would be some more news, but she was adamant that Robert was not to be disturbed with visitors this evening.

Merry put her arms around Toni, who had started to shiver. The closest place to stay would be her aunt and uncle's for the night, but when she suggested it, Toni became hysterical. She wasn't moving from the hospital until she had seen Robert!

So Merry sat with her arms around Toni in the small stuffy waiting room. The receptionist brought them in some sandwiches and coffee. Merry forced the hot drink into Toni and made sure she ate all the sandwiches. Then she went back to the car for Toni's soft woollen coat and prepared for a long and unpleasant wait through the night. She also didn't want to move from the hospital until she had spoken to Robert's eye specialist!

Chapter 13

When Merry opened her eyes the next morning, she stared blankly at the unfamiliar walls of the hospital waiting room. Memory returned with a dreadful rush.

She glanced at Toni, but she still slept, stretched along the bench, her dark hair falling across her face. *Some evening*, Merry thought wryly to herself. She stood up, yawned, and pushed her tangled hair out of her eyes. It had taken her a long time the night before to settle the almost hysterical Toni to calmness and reason. Merry had watched over her protectively, until she had collapsed into an exhausted sleep, and sheer tiredness caused her to nod off as well on the uncomfortable bench.

She looked at her watch and her eyes widened. They had both slept quite late! The hospital staff were bustling around and there was the hum of cleaners around the wards. The aroma of frying bacon and tomatoes drifted up the corridor. Merry suddenly realized that she was hungry. She shook Toni's shoulder gently.

Toni lifted her head and opened her eyes. For a few seconds they were blank, and then the dread and anguish crept back into them. Her lips quivered.

"He's died, hasn't he?" she whispered.

"I doubt it," Merry retorted in what she hoped was a good imitation of Aunt Adelaide's most bracing no-nonsense tone. "I should think if he's had a good night, we should be able to get in to see him this morning."

Toni sat up and swung her black hair out of her face, her eyes starting to shine.

"After we've had some breakfast and cleaned ourselves up," Merry warned. "We don't want to give him too much of a shock."

This argument seemed to work. After checking with the nurse that Mr. Tewne had had a comfortable night and perhaps they could see him for a few minutes after the specialist had visited, Merry was able to steer Toni out to the car.

They drove to the motel nearest the hospital and booked a room. Merry was thankful for her overnight case as they showered and freshened up. Afterwards, they found a cafe open and had breakfast.

"You are right, you know," Toni said cheerfully. "I feel better already. Do you think the reason he told his mother that he didn't want to see me was because he's worried about his sight?"

"It sounds like Robert,' Merry admitted cautiously.

"As if it would make any difference," Toni scoffed.

Merry was silent. She could understand Robert's despair, and she was doubtful that Robert would accept Toni back now. She kept her doubts to herself. Toni was much more cheerful this morning.

"The specialist was due at the hospital at ten," Toni prompted. She was starting to get nervous again. "We should get back!"

However, it was a long two hours wait before the specialist had got around to examining Robert and allowed himself to be stopped for his verdict.

"I can't promise anything," he said shortly, after Merry had introduced Toni as Mr. Tewne's fiancée and herself as his cousin. "If there are no setbacks, his eyes will probably be all right, but it is too soon to be absolutely sure about anything."

After he had hurried off, the nursing sister took pity on them. "You can go in one at a time," she promised. "Only for a few minutes. He does have to be kept very quiet."

Merry looked at Toni, but she pushed Merry ahead of her. "Please tell him I'm sorry and I love him," she pleaded. "And ask if he will see..." her voice faltered. "Let me come in," she corrected.

Merry followed the nurse past the big ward and through the door into the small room. Robert was a motionless cocoon held together on the high hospital bed by a network of ropes and pulleys. She recognized his nose and the bitter twist of his mouth under the masking bandages. The nurse took his hand and squeezed it gently.

"Mr. Tewne," she said quietly. "Your cousin Merry has come in to see you for a few minutes."

"Merry?" he said quietly.

Merry moved closer to the bed and reached to hold his hand. "You look a mess! Can I ask how you are feeling?"

"A mess," he said cheerfully.

"Toni is waiting outside to see you," Merry continued. Her heart sank as his smile faded and the bitter twist came back to his mouth. "She sent in a message that she is sorry and that she loves you." Robert remained silent. Merry tried again. "She said that she is sorry for what she did."

"A bit late," Robert said wearily. "And, Merry, my love, keep your nose out of my affairs. Right out of them," he warned. "Toni is an amusing little piece, but right now I'm not in the mood for her amusements."

"You're not going to see her?"

"Hardly," he sneered back.

The hovering nurse looked at her watch and pointed to the door.

"Is there anything you want me to do?" Merry asked

"I did warn my mother that I don't want visitors, and she was supposed to keep her mouth shut about my whereabouts," Robert said with a sigh. "Not even you, Merry. Goodbye!"

Merry gave his hand one last squeeze and left the room. The lump in her throat made it difficult for her to speak. It was dreadful to see her easy-going cousin so implacably bitter. Toni took one look at her face and the shine died out of her eyes, leaving them curiously dead and flat.

"He is being pigheaded, isn't he?" she accused.

Merry nodded.

Toni sat slowly back on the bench staring straight ahead. "I don't blame him," she said miserably. "I have behaved like a spoilt, corrupt little bitch. I just didn't realize..." her voice tailed off. She looked up at Merry's pitying eyes and shrugged. "Don't look so sorry for me," she said defiantly. "It's only what I deserved after all! Who would have thought that Robert, of all people, would have such high principles?"

"It might only be the accident and that he's worried about being blind," Merry said gently. "Wait until he's feeling better, and we'll try again."

"It's not the accident. He's just pigheaded," Toni explained as she stood up. She was looking thoughtful, and her lips were compressed together tightly. She looked at Merry and squared her shoulders. "I'll drive you home. At least I know where he is, and that he is almost all right and I have to thank you for that."

The drive home was accomplished in silence. Toni drove steadily and carefully. She was looking more and more thoughtful, and there was a determined set to her mouth. The misery and uncertainty were gone, and she seemed resolute and almost confident.

Merry, tired and depressed as she remembered the bitter twist to Robert's mouth and the uncertainty of whether he would regain his sight, felt little inclination to say anything. If Robert had warned his mother that he didn't want any contact with anyone, no one could risk visiting him. Whatever he was suffering, he was going to ride out alone, without help or support. She thought of the expensive specialist and her worry eased a fraction. His parent's money would ensure the best of medical attention for him, despite his rejection of them.

"Are you going to tell your people?" Toni asked, breaking their long silence as she slowed to a stop in front of Merry's house

"If I tell them, they might pass it on to Sean," Merry said glumly. "And Robert doesn't want anyone to know what's happened."

"Some evening we had," Toni sighed. Her face changed at Merry's desolate expression. She put out her hand and grasped Merry's warmly. "It wasn't your fault! I really am grateful for your support."

Merry remembered her earlier fears about Toni passing on Robert's whereabouts.

"You won't say anything to anybody, will you?" she demanded. It would have seemed too much like tempting fate to mention Sean Westwood by name.

"Look! What I've got to do, I've got to do by myself!" Toni said forthrightly. "It's nothing for you to worry about, and Robert won't suffer from it I promise you."

It was an explanation that left Merry bewildered and despite the reassurance, angry. Was Toni going to go back on her desperate promise not to tell Sean? She lifted her case from the car with an angry abruptness.

"Trust me!" Toni pleaded. "And don't ever worry about Sean! Just don't tell him anything about Robert. I can handle things my own way." Then she drove off.

"Why didn't Toni come in for some lunch?" her aunt grumbled. "I set an extra place when I saw you both arrive. How was the evening?"

"Interesting, but I think she was in a hurry to get back," Merry explained.

She looked around the familiar living room; at her father sprawled back in his chair immersed in his orchid magazine and her aunt carving the inevitable Sunday roast. Her aunt looked at them both, and they sat down and started eating.

She felt as if she had been missing for years instead of just overnight. Too much had happened in too short a time. She had discovered that she actually liked Toni and that Robert, her easy-going cousin was respected by Toni for his high principles!

"Such a nice girl, that Toni Gamberton," her aunt continued. "Bill and Marilyn are so thrilled that Robert is marrying such a very suitable young girl."

"Yes," Merry discovered in surprise. "She is nice! I think that she has a lot of character, even if she had been spoilt by her parents." She paused and thought about what she had said.

"And did you see Sean last night?" Aunt Adelaide asked, almost as if her question was triggered off by Merry's thoughts. "He said he was going straight down to Toni's place last night."

"He was here yesterday?" Merry gasped.

Her father looked up from his dinner. "And he had sent you the first blooms of his hybrids," he laughed. "Told you so!"

"He was disappointed that he had missed the pair of you," Aunt Adelaide rambled on. "But he said that he would catch up with you."

Merry stopped eating as the implication of what her aunt had said sunk in. Sean would now know that she and Toni hadn't arrived at her place for the evening and, of course, that there was no kitchen tea evening for the non-existent engagement!

"You're looking pale, Merry," her father remarked. "All this racketing around is too much for you. Try and have a rest this afternoon."

Merry agreed, glad to have an excuse for the refuge of her room. Later that afternoon when she had rejoined them, the sight of the grey Mercedes turning into their driveway was enough to cause her precipitate flight back to the refuge of her bedroom, with the excuse of a sudden headache. Although, she thought desperately to herself, as she listened to the low murmur of conversation from the living room, she was going to have trouble dodging Sean if he was really determined to see her.

The next week passed quickly. Merry started to relax. The sunny weather was lasting and so was the frantic rush of business. They were almost too busy even to talk, much to Merry's secret relief. Her Aunt Adelaide was still watching her carefully and not saying anything.

Merry made a furtive phone call to her aunt one night. The guarded news was that Robert's sight was going to be all right.

"Still be another week before the bandages come off," her aunt had quavered. "But they are confident there are not going to be any problems, thank God!"

The heavy load of depression Merry carried immediately lifted. She regained her zest for flower arranging. No one seemed to have seen Sean and the nice young man from the other office was still checking stores and collecting the takings. Two more of the pink hybrid orchids arrived for her during the week, still with no note or explanation, and the little apprentice's tendency to giggle became more pronounced each time.

Merry worked late on the Saturday afternoon again. This time she had to decorate a private home for the wedding reception. She was just leaving when the wedding party arrived back. She paused to admire them and the wistful feeling crept over her again.

The bride was pretty, and the groom adoring, and their love and happiness was a tangible, obvious thing. The bouquets she had made up, she was pleased to see, exactly matched the pink of the bridesmaids' dresses.

"A very pretty wedding," murmured a voice at her shoulder.

"Yes," she breathed. Then she realized the voice was familiar. It was Sean, sombre in well-cut grey business suit. "What are you doing here?" she demanded.

"Just passing," he explained. "I thought this might have been your last stop." Merry opened up the door of the Mini to leave, but he pushed it shut again. "I seem to have trouble catching up with you."

"Well, you have caught up with me," Merry retorted, and then remembered her manners. "Thank you for the orchids. Your hybrid strain looks fabulous." She sneaked a look at his face. "Is there a problem?" she ventured.

"I don't believe so," he said. "I really only wanted to reassure you. It makes it very awkward to talk business with a gazetted business partner who scurries out of my way like a disappearing mouse all the time."

"What was the business you wanted to discuss, and shouldn't we run a meeting with Dad present?" Merry asked, irked by his subtle allusion to her cowardice.

"This wasn't concerning your father," he said. He flicked at a speck of dust at the side of his dark jacket. "I thought you would be relieved to know that the money has been returned."

"I'm glad that you are no longer out of pocket," Merry said stiffly. Curiosity impelled the next question. "Who returned it?"

"Bill Townsend, with apologies for the delay," he drawled.

Merry took a deep breath of relief. So, Robert had stopped being pigheaded and told his father what he wanted the money for and his father had paid it across. Sean's presence was forgotten as she stood and thought.

If this was the reason that Toni had broken her engagement, surely she and Robert would now be reconciled? The money was paid back! Surely there was now no reason for the bitterness between them anymore? She smiled. When she got home, she would ring Toni and sound out exactly what was happening. She tried to open the car door, but Sean held it shut.

"You didn't get to Toni's non-existent kitchen tea?" he asked mildly.

"My movements are no business of yours," Merry protested.

She stared straight at him, wondering if Toni had told him where Robert was. Not that it mattered now she thought and smiled her satisfaction. The money was paid!

"Of course not," he drawled. "It was just that the coincidence had me curious--you missing on Saturday night. Exactly how charming and persuasive were you to get the money returned by this week?"

Merry listened to him in bewilderment. He was unaware that Robert was hospitalized, but he had worked out that they were probably together. Suddenly she realized what he was insinuating! Her face flamed, and the blue of her eyes blazed into brilliance.

The group of people laughing and talking on the porch of the big house turned in surprise at the loud sound of the slap. However, there was only a small blue Mini driving away at a dangerous speed and a tall well-dressed man entering his Mercedes.

Chapter 14

"Merry!" Aunt Adelaide broke the habit of years as she entered Merry's bedroom without knocking. "What is wrong?"

Merry kept her tearstained face hidden in the pillow. "Go away," she wept. "I don't want to talk to anyone."

Her aunt sat beside her and patted her on the shoulder. After a while Merry's sobs lessened and then stopped. Her aunt still didn't say anything.

Merry sat up and blew her nose. "He's the most detestable person that I have ever met," she ground out. "I'm never going to speak to him again!"

"You have had a fight with Sean?" her aunt guessed.

"You don't understand," Merry said indignantly.

Her aunt waited, but Merry lapsed back into resentful silence. She couldn't tell her aunt the whole story without involving Robert. And if her aunt really knew what had happened, the brunt of her disapproval would fall on Robert, not Sean!

"It doesn't matter," Merry said as she blew her nose.

She also couldn't ask her maiden aunt's advice about the passionate abandon that Sean's kisses aroused in her, despite the way he infuriated her so much. She remembered with wistful envy the love and tenderness that had surrounded that last bridal couple like a visible aura.

If only she could make up her mind about whether she loved or hated Sean Westwood! He made her feel like a yo-yo, she thought resentfully. Her undisciplined emotions were muddling up her thinking and complicating her life.

"I think that you need a nice hot cup of tea and an aspirin, my girl," her aunt decided.

Merry tried to smile. It was a wry smile, but it was definitely a smile. "Your solutions to all the problems of life, Aunt Adelaide."

She swung into the bathroom to splash cold water on her swollen eyes. From now on she promised, as she held the wet flannel against the puffiness around her eyes, she would behave like a lady and never lose her temper again! Sean was never going to discover the way he made her feel.

No one sighted him the next week, but on the Monday a small posy of pink roses arrived for Merry, no note or card attached. On Tuesday, it was a spray of vivid orange orchids. On Wednesday it was a spray of tiny multi coloured miniature roses. By Thursday their deliveryman had a broad grin on his face as he delivered the now familiar white box with the miniature red roses nestled inside. On Friday the package held another spray of the pink orchids.

Aunt Adelaide stopped working to admire them, but again made no comment. Sylvia grinned as broadly as the deliveryman did at the regularity of the arrival of the flowers. Merry put the orchids in a vase, and they joined the rest of the row of vases on the back shelf.

Merry glared at Sylvia, who suddenly got busy with the boxes of seedlings. Her aunt concentrated on the docket book and avoided her accusing eye. Merry let out her breath in an exasperated sigh. She knew perfectly well that the flowers were arriving from Sean! His nurseries were the only place where the hybrid orchids could come from. Yet without a card or a note, she couldn't officially return them. She even wished he would turn up, so she could demand an explanation, but there was no sign of him.

She rang her Aunt Marilyn, who said that Robert was out of hospital, and that his eyes were all right. She explained that Toni had managed to reconcile Robert and his father, and that they were talking of getting married as soon as Robert was off his crutches.

"Weddings are contagious, you know," she chattered on. "I suppose that you and Sean will be setting a date soon?"

"Don't get your hopes up," Merry warned. She tried to keep a light and humorous note in her voice. "Sean and I aren't getting along that well."

"Lover's tiffs," her aunt dismissed. "I will be so disappointed if your lovely wedding dress doesn't get used."

"Give my love to Robert and Toni," Merry said and hung up on her aunt thoughtfully.

So Toni had somehow managed to get Robert to forgive her, and was now officially engaged again! It was wonderful news that he was going to be all right. It was equally wonderful that after all these years she had managed to reconcile Robert with his father!

On the Sunday, it was a magnificent day with a cloudless blue sky, and enough cool breeze to keep the temperature down. Her restlessness intensified.

"Think I'll go for a drive and maybe drop in on Aunt Marilyn and Uncle Bill. Either of you want to come?"

"I'm going over to the nursery," her father apologized. "Bit worried about the humidity control."

"Some other time, perhaps," her aunt promised. "I've arranged to go with the floral exhibition with Mrs. Warne."

Merry backed the Mini out and drove off. There was a lot of traffic on the road, and she had to concentrate on her driving until she was on the freeway. There was always the chance that her aunt and uncle wouldn't be home, but she felt that she needed to get away. It would probably be better; she fumed to herself, if her father and aunt would only say something instead of always watching her in such an understanding silence!

She pulled into the courtyard of Winterview beside the red Lamborghini. The familiar grey Mercedes was parked beside it. She sat in her car and looked at it. Did she want to see Sean again? What was he doing here? Would it be better to turn tail and come back some other time? However, the front door opened, and her aunt came running out to the car to pull Merry out and hug her.

"In you come," she said with a beaming smile. "Robert and Toni are here and your Sean as well."

"He's not my Sean," Merry protested.

Sean sprawled on the high-backed armchair beside her uncle, who beamed his pleasure at seeing her. Merry smiled at everyone. She decided that Robert's description of his parents as 'that sour faced couple' hardly fitted any more. She had never seen her aunt and uncle look so happy.

A radiant Toni nestled beside Robert. Behind his dark glasses, Merry could see the satisfaction and contentment on his face. There were crutches resting against the side of his chair, but no other evidence of his dreadful accident.

"If it isn't my favourite kissing cousin," he said with a wide grin.

"You look a lot less of a mess," Merry laughed as she came over and kissed him. "I believe that congratulations are in order?"

"Just the person I wanted to see," Toni said breathlessly. "Will you be my bridesmaid? Please, Merry? We are organizing the wedding in six weeks' time. Robert will be rid of the crutches by then."

"Love to," Merry agreed.

"Jerry is going to be best man and Sean the groomsman," Toni continued.

Merry sneaked a look at Sean, who watched her gravely. She realized that as Toni's cousin he was the obvious choice for groomsman. The conversation flowed on, about venues and clothes and guests. Eventually her uncle produced a bottle of champagne.

"Just a small drink to celebrate," he chuckled. "We have a lot to celebrate and be thankful for--Robert's home safe and sound and we have a new member of the family to welcome here."

The glasses were filled. "To Robert and Toni" was the toast, as they drank to the happy couple.

"And to Uncle Bill," Toni returned, raising her glass high. "For being the most wonderful and understanding new father a girl could have."

Merry was amused to see that this toast was greeted with equal enthusiasm by Robert. Toni had certainly worked a miracle by healing the breach between Robert and his father, she decided, as she watched him raise his glass to his father with such an open look of pleasure on his face.

She raised her own glass towards Toni. "To the peacemaker," she said impulsively.

"Some peacemaker," Robert teased as he kissed his fiancée, "Uses a pretty heavy club to bludgeon us all into submission."

"A forty-five thousand dollar club," Toni said smugly.

There was suddenly a silence. Sean stared at Toni with a look of disgust. Merry's aunt looked puzzled, and her uncle both amused and embarrassed.

"What?" Sean demanded sharply.

"Leave it, Toni," Robert ordered grimly.

Toni just dimpled up and laughed. "Look at the expression on Sean's face," she giggled. "Steady, stodgy and reliable Sean! The all knowing, all wise, all efficient company director has missed something hasn't he?"

"Of course, it is going to be difficult," Robert warned. "But I suppose I could still spank you with one of my crutches if you don't shut up."

"Merry's entitled to know, she's family," Toni said defiantly. "And if Sean knows," a definitely malicious smile curved her lips, "that might make him family as well."

"If you don't tell me what I should know, it won't be Robert who beats you with the crutches," Sean threatened.

Toni backed against her future father-in-law. "I stole the money, and Robert took the blame," she said baldly. She laughed at Sean's face. "It wasn't such a dreadful thing after all! I mean, Daddy has shares worth twice that amount in the company."

"You stole the money!" Sean repeated blankly. His face faded to a dirty grey and there was a look of horror in his eyes.

"It paid for our half share on the yacht we're going to go cruising in," Toni explained. "Only Robert refused to go along with it and tried to break our engagement."

"A man of principle," his father said with a smile.

Suddenly, the missing pieces fell into place. Because Robert always seemed so casual about everything, Toni had assumed that he would go along with her theft. She didn't consider it theft because her father had so much money in the company, but Robert did! He had shouldered the blame and went off to earn enough money to repay it! No wonder the spoilt Toni was so distracted.

"What about your own parents?" Merry asked. "Would they have paid it for you?'

"You took the company for forty-five thousand and then expected your father to pay another forty-five thousand?" Sean gasped.

"Robert had decided that it was a family matter as it was his fiancée," Merry's uncle explained. "And you know how pigheaded Robert is."

"We know," Merry and Aunt Marilyn chorused.

"I confessed to Uncle Bill that Robert had had this dreadful accident trying to repay the money I took, and was actually standing on his dignity, his integrity and his honour and refusing to marry me as well. So, Uncle Bill paid it out," Toni explained, smiling up into the indulgent face of her future father-in-law.

"The money wasn't important," Uncle Bill said with a shrug. "They are both welcome to whatever is around." He looked again at his son and pride glowed in his eyes. "I'm only glad that Toni had the guts to confess to me. I discovered that I don't mind at all having a pigheaded and honourable son." He tried for a lighter touch. "We might have had a breach of promise suit on our hands."

"Definitely," Toni said with a chuckle. "I had no intention of letting my most noble fiancé slide out of my clutches."

"I should still beat you to a pulp with that crutch," Sean threatened, although his eyes were dancing. "I can't see how anyone can forgive you for what you did."

"I must be the forgiving type," Robert drawled. "Besides she's going to promise to love and honour me in a few weeks and I am trying to get the 'obey' put back into the service."

This set off a round of mirth. Merry sneaked a look at her watch.

"Do you have to go right now?" her aunt wailed, interpreting the look. "What about staying for dinner?"

"I don't like driving after dark," Merry apologized. "Not in the Mini."

"I'll drive you back afterwards," Sean offered.

"I have to get the Mini home anyway," Merry said awkwardly, not looking at Sean. She tried for a lighter note. "Westwood and Merriland's will be doing all the flowers for this wedding, remember!"

This set off the mirth again. Merry kissed Robert and Toni, her aunt and uncle, and nodded an airy farewell in Sean's direction, and left in a chorus of good wishes and good-byes.

The warm glow lasted Merry all the way home. She kept seeing Robert's boyishly contented face as he watched his fiancée. Everything had turned out nicely. She suspected it would be a while before Toni dared cross Robert again, after nearly losing him. Also, although she didn't really care, she was glad that the suspicion of her complicity in the theft was over. For a few seconds, Sean had looked almost stricken when he had discovered the truth!

"That Toni will settle him down," Aunt Adelaide remarked when Merry reached home and passed on the news of the wedding. "Such a nice young girl."

It was after dinner that the ring on the front door came. Merry saw her aunt and father, who had seemed very quiet and pre-occupied during dinner, exchange glances.

"Visitors at this hour," Merry sighed as she went to answer the door. She almost closed it when she realized who the visitor was, but Sean had stepped inside.

"Hello, Tom, Miss Land," he said.

He stood aside as they both stood up and walked through the door past him.

"Where are you both going?" Merry asked suspiciously.

"An after-dinner stroll," her father explained.

"Just for half an hour," Aunt Adelaide promised. She took her brother's arm and they walked off together down the darkened street.

"You set this up, didn't you?" Merry accused.

Sean closed the door behind him and propelled Merry into the living room. He sat down on the couch, and casually pulled Merry on to his knee and held her tightly. "I rang them to give me time to have an uninterrupted talk with you."

"Why should I want to talk to you?" Merry demanded, averting her gaze from the unsettling effect of the golden lights dancing in his grey eyes. She sensed his nearness having its predictable effect on her. She had to tense herself against the insidious pull her body was making towards him.

"You have a financial interest in our company," Sean murmured in her ear. "Do you realize what it is going to cost Westwood and Merriland's if I have to send you flowers every day for the rest of your life, because you won't accept my apology?"

Merry felt her pulse begin to beat faster. To her annoyance, she felt the hot colour rise into her cheeks. She knew exactly what she had to do. She had to behave in a ladylike and dignified manner and keep him at a distance.

"It's accepted," she replied. "Now, please let me go."

"For all the dreadful things I thought and said to you," he insisted, still holding her tightly. "I admit I deserved to have my ears boxed for the way I have treated you."

"Yes," Merry said.

"Toni was right, you know. I would like the chance to become a part of the family. When I thought you were going to marry Robert..." He tightened his arms around her. "It was a bridal outfit, wasn't it? Why did you buy it?"

Merry remained silent. Sean turned her head around to face him.

"Am I going to be allowed to propose without having my ears boxed yet again?" he asked meekly.

Merry looked directly at him. His eyes were steady, honest and searching, but it was the hint of anxiety as he waited for her answer, that caused the glow to spread through her, so that she relaxed more comfortably into his arms.

She would make up a spray she thought dreamily, to match the hand-painted flowers on the skirt of her ideal wedding dress.

"As long as you don't have any ambitions about having the word 'obey' put back into the service," she warned.

"Sounds ominous!" he groaned. "Do you realize I have been trying to pluck up courage to propose to you practically since the start of the partnership?" His mouth touched her face. "Let me hear you accept properly," he prompted.

"I accept your proposal," she said primly. "I don't want you to send the company into receivership over your extravagance."

His lips lowered on to hers. The familiar lassitude crept through her, and she put her arms around him. This time however, there was no dreadful inner turmoil as she abandoned herself to returning his kisses. Her rebellious mind had at last come to terms with her passionately loving heart.

The end

You can find ALL our books up on our website at:

http://www.writers-exchange.com

All our romances:

http://www.writers-exchange.com/category/genres/romance/

All Jacquelyn's Books:

http://www.writers-exchange.com/Jacquelyn-Webb/

About the Author

Jacquelyn Webb is the pen name for multi-genre writing Margaret Pearce.

Margaret is a compulsive writer. She started off life as a copywriter and just kept on going, through marriage, children, Arts Degree at Monash and grandchildren. She lives a fairly secluded life in an underground flat in the Dandenongs in Victoria. Margaret cut her teeth on sci/fi and never quite recovered from it being her first love as a genre.

Check out all her books on her author page:

http://www.writers-exchange.com/Jacquelyn-Webb/

If you enjoyed this author's book, then please place a review up at the site of purchase, and any social media sites you frequent!

Hong Kong Stopover

Josie Sutherland is a computer journalist. Her quiet stopover in Hong Kong is thrown into chaos when she witnesses a failed robbery. She suspects the victim, Carey Court, is involved in software smuggling when they're both kidnapped, and the instant attraction between them complicates everything.

When they escape, Josie decides to masquerade as a drug courtier along with Carey to get the story she needs about software smuggling. Together, they move through an underworld of danger, intrigue and death where everyone's out to get them. The only truth in a dangerous, make-believe world is their feelings for one another...

Publisher: http://www.writers-exchange.com/Hong-Kong-Stopover/

Roses are for Romance

With her family florist business ailing, Merry agrees to a merger with a former rival and quickly learns to resent her new, gorgeous, partner Sean Westwood, who tramples over nearly all of her decisions, especially those concerning her irresponsible blind eye to her charming cousin Robert.

When Robert vanishes along with their money, Merry's frantic search for him causes Sean to assume she's Robert's accomplice. Caught between half-truths and evasions, Merry struggles to ignore her growing attraction to Sean. Learning to trust a man she's refused to see as her savior since he bailed out her ruined company may be the key to unlocking the mystery of Robert's disappearance...and her own heart.

Publisher: http://www.writers-exchange.com/roses-are-for-romance/

If you want to read more about other Romance novels by this publisher, they are listed on...

http://www.writers-exchange.com/category/genres/romance/

You can find ALL our books on our website at:

http://www.writers-exchange.com

All our romances:

http://www.writers-exchange.com/category/genres/romance/

All Jacquelyn's Books:

http://www.writers-exchange.com/Jacquelyn-Webb/